SIGNAL ON THE HILL

A Cole Williams Novel

by

Brian Boland

Also by Brian Boland

CARIBBEAN'S KEEPER: A NOVEL OF VENDETTA
GRAVES IN THE SAND: A COLE WILLIAMS NOVEL

Mother, mother ocean,
I have heard your call.
Wanted to sail upon your waters
since I was three feet tall.

—*A Pirate Looks at Forty*

CHAPTER 1 – GEORGE STREET

THE COLD AND DARK claws of winter gripped tight against what should have by now been the first fleeting indications of the spring season. It was late March, yet the unpredictable winter wind, prone as it always was to violent fits, still hurled itself down side streets and collided like a drunken fool against the tightly packed buildings of downtown. When the wind blew like this, the late afternoon morphed seamlessly with the early evening. The temperature seemed to fall off a cliff at the very moment the sun disappeared over the distant jagged west coast of Newfoundland. To the casual observer, the winter days were often dismal as clouds, fog, and heavy snow fought and blurred the otherwise stunning landscape. Nighttime brought with it a seemingly unbearable cold, yet somehow the hearty people of this defiant town had persisted throughout the centuries. Boldly standing its ground against the bitter North Atlantic, the people of St. John's dug in for another night and waited patiently for the storm to pass.

Cole sat alone against a stone wall. Smoke-stained wooden rafters hung precariously low over his head, while heavy dark wooden stools, most empty, sat evenly spaced around the length of the bar, where he rested with his forearms dug in hard against the weathered wood. In what had perhaps become his favorite barstool in all of Newfoundland, he was content to be tucked in among the shadows well enough that other patrons rarely noticed him until their second, third, or tenth round. Halfway through his second pint of whatever stout beer had been poured for him, the chills that shook his shoulders finally subsided. He didn't recognize the bartender and, cute as she was, he was disappointed.

Isabella had left with Marie that morning during a lull in the weather when it looked like some flights would make it out. It was supposed to have been a two-week visit, but she'd come up with a good reason for their early departure. Her father was ill, or so she had said. Cole took a sip and didn't blame her. He was thankful she'd recognized the awkwardness of their visit or perhaps even the slow unspoken tension that had been building for the five days she'd been with him in Newfoundland. At present, the void in his chest was paired with the sad knowledge that he had no one to blame but himself. She had hugged him at the airport, a hug that lasted seconds longer than he thought it would. He knew that she loved him in some fucked up kind of way, but for him there were still lingering traces of some physical and emotional attraction that seemed to eat away at any progress the two of them ever made in establishing even the most basic level of a functioning relationship. *It was good she left,* he thought.

Marie was nearing two years old, and he'd played with her on the floor of Tony's rented house nearly every waking minute of each day while they'd been there. Cole had made plans for each day, but the weather had all but ruined each of them. Nevertheless, Isabella had been content to rest, relax, and give Cole as much time as possible with his little girl. They'd gone walking one morning when the sun briefly escaped from behind the heavy low clouds, and Cole wondered if that wasn't where the trouble had started. They'd hiked the road up to Signal Hill and at the top, overlooking a heavy fog bank over the Atlantic Ocean that sat several hundred feet below, he felt the unmistakable onset of a deep sadness. Surely Isabella with her quick intuition had caught on to it. They were pretending things were normal, but each knew they were not.

It was good she left, he told himself once more, a mantra that, at that moment, he thought wise to hold onto. No hope was left for them to ever rekindle the romance that had started so far away on Martinique. His failed attempt at a normal life in Normandy had been cut short and sealed their tragic fate. In a moment of misplaced grandiosity, he thought his story to be almost Shakespearean. The life he'd wanted with Isabella was nothing more than smoke lifted and carried by the aimless wind that was his life and to chase it was an exercise in futility. Isabella knew it to be true and her decision to leave was a merciful act on her part to not let things unravel any further between the two of them and the daughter they shared. He loved her still, in some indescribable way now devoid of physical affection, yet at the same time he wished for nothing but the best for her, and for Marie.

He hadn't cried when he passed Marie off to Isabella at the airport. That, more than anything else, was on his mind as he got down to the last two warm sips of his beer and nodded at the bartender for another. After Isabella had left, he'd taken a cab back to Tony's house, a small cottage perched on the Battery cliffs just inside the mouth of the bay. Standing at the front door, despite the wind and the incessant cold, Cole had turned and walked for downtown, taking a meandering path down by the docks then up towards George Street and finally to his favorite barstool. Now he sat as the bartender brought him a third stout, and Cole took a long sip. She turned back to the bar without even a smile. Since he'd last looked around, a group had gathered at one of the far tables in the corner of the UnderBelly. All at once, with the new company, he felt the urge to leave and finished his beer quickly before settling his tab and walking back up the winding stairs to the main restaurant. The YellowBelly, situated on the street level, afforded a slightly brighter atmosphere, and the tables were now full of couples and friends eating dinner on an otherwise bitter evening.

There was a part of him that wanted companionship like all of those happy people around him. Yet he also wore an immense sadness like a damp coat over his shoulders and knew that solitude suited him far better on a night like this. Cole walked quickly out and around the bar to the front door, and felt himself almost knocked against the outer wall when the wind first grabbed hold of him. The beer kept him warm enough and his belly full, so he walked alone under the streetlights for some time more.

———

He awoke in the morning, having passed out on Tony's couch. As his eyes opened, he knew immediately that he'd drank whiskey and cursed at himself. Beer was fun, rum was fun, but whiskey was the devil's drink of choice. He tried not to move, but felt the room spinning before he could even close his eyes again. Tony was cooking breakfast in the kitchen.

"You know you can sleep in your room, right?"

Cole ignored him.

Tony persisted, "You look like shit." He paused, "Again."

"Thanks, Tony. I was going to ask you what you thought of my outfit."

Cole rolled onto his back, his eyes still shut, until he smelled coffee. Tony had been, as always, kind to him. True to his word, he'd offered Cole a place to stay while the dust settled from Mexico. Cole secretly reckoned he was also most likely now on the Virginia State Police shit list, so he'd had little choice but to take Tony up on the offer. St. John's was an ideal spot to lay low. Tony had been there since they'd last met in France, his mission not entirely known to Cole, but the work was easy. They took turns sitting for hours at a spotting scope with a high power camera perched next to them. From the living room window, Tony had a commanding view of the entrance to the harbor and at seemingly random times either him or Cole stood a constant watch. When a certain fishing boat—or even at times a sailboat—came in or out, they clicked away at the camera and wrote detailed descriptions of the people onboard, numbers of antennas, registrations numbers, and just about every detail they could put down on paper. What Tony did with it, Cole wasn't exactly sure. Nevertheless, it was easy work for free room and board.

Cole had been on the couch while Isabella and Marie had visited. With no recollection of the previous evening, Cole surmised that he'd subconsciously preferred the couch over the bed where Isabella had slept the night before. Even with them gone, he wasn't particularly fond of the idea of going back in there. He slowly worked his way up to a sitting position, and Tony set a cup down in front of him. He took a slow sip and closed his eyes, trying for a moment to remember anything after the UnderBelly. From his pocket, he emptied out a handful of coins onto the table, along with an ATM receipt from George Street and some woman's name and number scribbled in black ink on a piece of paper adorned with the Delta Hotel stationary. *Trouble*, he thought.

He took another longer sip of the coffee and made his way over to the large window, looking out at the harbor. The weather was once again dog shit. A moderate snow blew sideways past the house and the sun tried its best to break through the low hanging clouds, but it would most certainly be another cloudy and cold day.

"We looking for anything today?"

Tony stopped chopping for a second and looked out the window before turning back to Cole, "Not today."

Two weeks before, he'd followed Tony to the airport after the sun had set. At what must have been a pre-arranged gate, Tony and Cole had slipped inside the fence line and Tony fastened some kind of tracking device inside a void on the rudder of a small twin-engine plane. It was the most exciting thing he'd done in the past four months. Tony hadn't said much about it since then, and Cole wondered about it on the long mornings and afternoons when the weather held them inside the small house.

"Anything with that plane?"

Tony looked at Cole again, this time with a smile, "What plane?"

Cole smiled and shook his head, which immediately reminded him of the hangover he'd managed to forget for the past two minutes. Finishing the coffee, he grabbed a pillow off the couch and made his was around to the back bedroom.

"I'm gonna sleep."

Tony didn't reply. Once inside the room, Cole felt sick to his stomach. It wasn't the whiskey, though; rather it was the faintest hint of Isabella and the thought of Marie that nearly took his legs out from underneath him. He drew the curtains to shut out what little light was outside and laid down on the cool sheets, pulling the thick blanket up to his neck, and rolled to his side. A single strand of hair was caught between his fingers, and he held it up to his face for a second. It was dark and slightly curled, too long to be Marie's.

Dammit, he thought. He wrapped it around his knuckles twice then gripped tight, feeling it cut into his skin before it snapped from the tension. Cole held his fist and grit his teeth. Shutting his eyes, he begged for sleep and focused on slowing his breathing. The house Tony rented was a bright shade of orange with white trim. A neat white picket fence lined the small yard, and a matching shed sat off to one side. The inside was painted in light shades of blue and green. It was a thing in Newfoundland to paint the houses in bright colors, perhaps to forget the darkness that hung over the town for so much of the year. Cole's room was a shade or two off from yellow and at that moment, as he lay there, he wished it was a dark shade of red or green. Pastels rarely matched his mood.

He lay still, his eyes closed, and as his breathing slowed he felt his brain settle. His mind wandered back to the night before, but the details were a blur after the UnderBelly. He laughed for a moment, thinking how much of a mess he must have been when whomever she was that had snagged him tried dragging him back to the Delta. With that, he remembered some faint chorus of a song and the rough outline of another dark bar materialized in his mind. The open chords of a guitar and the rhythmic beating of a bodhran grew louder as bits and pieces came together to form a partial memory. *It was a good song, if only I could remember it.* With that, Cole nodded off.

Tony woke him later that afternoon with a few knocks before he opened Cole's door and let some light in from the living room.

"Can you watch the channel for a bit?"

Cole rolled in his bed and took a long breath to steady his still-dizzy brain.

"I thought you said we weren't looking for anything."

"There may be a sailboat arriving. I need to run by the governor's office."

It was Cole's way of paying rent, and he never pushed back at anything Tony asked him to do. He rolled again, sat up, and reached blindly around for his shirt. Finding it on the floor, he stumbled across the room, blinking and nodding in response to Tony's inquisitive look.

He asked, "Where'd you go last night, anyhow?"

Cole proceeded straight to the kitchen and rounded up the necessities for a fresh pot of coffee.

"I don't really know. But I think I drank whiskey."

Tony laughed and walked for the front door, wrapping a scarf around his neck before pulling a heavy winter coat over his shoulders. He opened the door, and even from across the small room, Cole felt the surge of cold air. It awakened his senses and for a moment he felt better.

Tony looked back for a second. "I'll be back in a few hours. Grab some photos of anything coming in, take notes on any sailboats."

Cole replied nonchalantly, "Got it."

It was a fairly familiar routine by this point. Cole guessed that it was drugs, or people, or perhaps something more nefarious. Whatever it was, it was most certainly smuggling. Twice since he'd been there, Tony had shown interest in some of the boats. In his room, upstairs, he had a mildly complex array of computers and a few phones. In a corner sat a small floor safe. Cole was frustrated at times that Tony hadn't let him in on all the details, but at the same time he knew the rules. Cole's nature was to break rules whereas Tony, for the most part, did his best to follow them.

With a pot of coffee brewing in the kitchen, Cole settled in for a long afternoon. He spent several hours in silence, looking out the big glass window as the picturesque landscape in front of him appeared from time to time between the bands of snow. Two towering cliffs on each side of the narrow channel, each bathed in white, kept out much of the North Atlantic's furious sea. The wind whipped in hard and blew dwarfed whitecaps across the thin sliver of water that led into the bay. Squall lines blew in intermittently, and Cole found them calming to watch as the snow danced in random directions at the mercy of the wind. The big pane of glass shook at times with the heaviest gusts.

Tony was back about two hours later.

"You need a break?" he asked.

Cole shook his head to say no.

Shaking the snow off his jacket, Tony set his outer garments on some hooks by the door and proceeded into the kitchen where he went to work to put some kind of dinner together. Tony was about 15 or so years older than Cole, but as was so often the case, he began with his usual father-figure questions.

"Seriously, where'd you go last night?"

He mocked Tony's voice, "Seriously Tony, I don't fucking remember."

He didn't look back to see Tony's response, but he knew a disapproving look had spread across his face.

"Did you see that girl?"

Cole snapped, "What girl?"

"The bartender."

Cole grit his teeth and regretted, for the tenth time, that he'd even mentioned her to Tony.

"No, she wasn't working."

Silence followed, with Cole well aware that Tony was probably looking at him. Outside, another line of snow came down, this time in a calm wind. The heavy snowflakes drifted down gently and stacked up on themselves in the small yard outside. Beyond that, on the single lane road, streaks of white crisscrossed back and forth. The far cliffs on the south side of the bay were almost entirely obscured.

"I sailed in snow a few times. It ain't fun."

Cole was trying to change the subject and, for a second, it seemed to work.

"Was this back at the academy?"

"Yeah, early spring practices on the river. We used to have to sweep snow off the boats."

He thought back to those days, now the better part of a decade past, then tried not to get caught up in the details between then and now. For a moment, his mind was mired in the confusion of Cozumel, and Harley, and Claire, and the rest of it. He pushed those thoughts aside and focused again on the snow. The road was now covered in a thin blanket.

"Looks like this one might stick."

Tony turned the conversation back to its beginnings, and asked, "Do you know her name?"

"Olivia."

"So you've talked to her?"

It was comical how bad Tony was at trying to give advice. He sounded like an afterschool made-for-television special on talking to errant teenagers. Cole was angry for a second before the absurdity of it all made him laugh.

"What's so funny?" Tony asked.

"I appreciate you looking out for me. I really do, Tony."

With that, Tony went silent and focused on finishing up with whatever he was cooking in the kitchen. It was beginning to smell good, and Cole stared intently out the window as the last bits of daytime light reflected off the heavy snowflakes falling outside. As the afternoon turned to evening, Tony brought two heaping plates of fajitas over to the small table by the window. Cole's appetite returned almost immediately. It was grilled chicken, tortillas, onions, and peppers, served with a healthy dose of sour cream.

Cole turned to look at Tony for a second, and smiled. "Where'd you learn to cook like this, anyhow?"

Tony grinned as he sat, "Key West."

Cole caught the reference.

"That was a long time ago, wasn't it?"

Tony took his first big bite, chewed for a few moments, then replied, "Yeah. That was a different time, huh?"

Cole nodded and searched for the right words, but couldn't find them.

Tony asked, "So you wouldn't sail in this stuff?"

Cole shook his head. "Nah, numb fingers, numb feet, numb face, that kind of shit sucks."

Tony had a sly smile on his face when he asked, "What if you had a few dozen kilos of coke with you?"

Cole laughed. It was the first genuine humor he'd felt that day, and his mind was flooded with thoughts, some good and some bad. He looked back at Tony, all at once immensely grateful for his friendship.

Casually, he replied, "There are always exceptions."

CHAPTER 2 – HARBOUR DRIVE

TONY HAD ROUSED Cole at a little past two in the morning. He'd slept for a good six hours, and as he quickly rolled over and sat up, he yawned once before pulling a sweatshirt over his head and getting up to his feet. Walking out of his room, he poured a large mug of coffee and took a sip. The room was dark with the only light sneaking in from the streetlight outside and the stars above. Cole looked for a moment more, trying to remember the last time he'd seen a clear sky. He then looked down and to his left at that narrow channel below.

"Anything?"

Tony was putting a few things away in the kitchen and brewing another pot of coffee for Cole. He continued with his work and spoke softly, "Nah, not a thing. Wake me up for any sailboats, OK?"

Cole took another sip and nodded to himself in the darkness. Tony was up the stairs less than a minute later. The floorboards creaked for another minute more before going entirely silent. It had been a long night. The hardest part of this work was staying awake. Daylight was another four or five hours away. Cole reckoned that if the clouds stayed away, it would be one hell of a sunrise, the kind that would lift his spirits. He stirred a spoonful of sugar into his coffee and took a seat by the spotting scope, kicking the chair onto its two back legs, and waited.

An hour passed with nothing. Cole walked to the front door and gently turned the knob. He felt the crisp air as soon as the door moved an inch. Opening it fully, he stepped out onto the porch, his bare feet in almost three inches of fresh snow. It burned at the soles of his feet. He took long breaths of the air, the steam rolling out of his mouth and into the darkness all around him. He was unable to shift his gaze away from the stars. The high moon was half full and reflected in flickers of bright light off the almost calm water below. As a minute passed, he felt the cold gnawing at his head, as if his skull was ensnarled in a vice. Still, he took more breaths and smiled. He hoped to get out of the house today.

Back inside, he dried his feet with a towel by the door and went back to his seat. The bitter cold had served its purpose, and he was now fully awake, aware of his surroundings, and feeling far better than he had in the past 24 hours. He was consumed by an introspective series of thoughts, as if the change in weather brought with it some new clarity about his life. He thought that perhaps his emotions might finally take a turn towards normalcy. They may very well have, had it not been for the boat that slowly stalked its way up and into the channel.

Cole squinted at first, unsure of what he was looking at. He lowered his head down to the scope and stared intently. She was nearly 40 feet long, a sloop, and clearly poorly kept. Her deck was a mess, and the sails were haphazardly furled, the boom swinging from side to side with the small gentle swell that rolled in amid the cliffs. Cole went to the camera next and snapped a few shots, but knew they'd be all-but-worthless in the darkness. As the boat chugged along at no more than four or five knots, he ran up to wake Tony. Two loud knocks at the door were all it took, and he heard Tony up and moving.

The two of them met downstairs again half a minute later, giving Tony enough time to get a good look at her stern. He rubbed at his chin a bit and scrolled through the photos Cole had snapped.

He asked, "Dirty?"

Cole shrugged. "It's four in the morning, and he doesn't have a single light on."

Tony nodded. "OK. Get dressed."

Cole put on the warmest clothes he could find and pulled his old leather boots out from under the bed. They weren't the ideal footwear for snow and ice, but he'd rubbed enough mink oil into them over the past few months to get them as close to waterproof as they ever would be. Tony was on the phone and motioned to Cole to head for the door.

Once outside, Tony hung up, and the two made for his truck. It rumbled along down Water Street, then on towards Harbour Drive before Tony parked a few blocks back from the concrete wharf. From there, they walked down the iced and slippery empty roads in the last half hour of darkness until they saw the boat again, idling up to tie up in between two hulking commercial fishing boats.

A moment later, the police began to materialize. Two came from the far end of the wharf, another four from across Harbour Drive, and several more hung back as a secondary perimeter. A Customs car came quickly from further downtown, its siren blaring. As it did, several shadows appeared for a moment from behind a building and took off running at a full sprint up the hill and away from the wharf. Several cops followed. By now, the first police to arrive had boarded the boat, and soon the two occupants were escorted off in handcuffs.

Cole and Tony watched in silence. More police cars appeared, and within 20 minutes, it seemed that every law-enforcement agency and vehicle on the island of Newfoundland was within a two block radius. A gruff man in jeans and a heavy winter coat approached them both, extending his hand to Tony.

He spoke with a thick Newfie accent, the 'h' in his words masked entirely by the 't.' "Thanks for the tip." He didn't seem entirely happy. "Might I ask what you were doing up at four in the morning?"

Tony smiled, "Nothing much, just a concerned resident of this fine city, Carl."

They shook firmly and Tony turned to introduce Cole. Carl extended his hand as well, smiling, but his face at the same time couldn't mask his uncertainty, and some level of discomfort, surrounding Cole's presence.

"This is Cole, a friend of mine from back in the States."

His beady eyes staring intently at Cole, Carl replied with a nod. "Pleasure to meet you, Cole."

Tony turned back towards the boat.

"So, what's the story?"

Carl spun back towards the wharf, dug his hands deep into his jacket pockets to shield them from the chill, and took a long breath.

"There's a few bundles that were buried under a pile of shit. About five, I'd say they're kilos, but we'll get it tested." Carl paused again. "What were you really doing up this early?"

Tony looked at Cole and flexed his eyebrows while Carl was still looking away towards the boat.

"Couldn't sleep, I guess."

Carl changed the subject. "How long are you staying for, Cole?"

"Dunno. Just starting to get into a kind of rhythm."

The three of them were silent for a few moments. Cole stared up again at the sky and took a breath to let the cold bite at his nostrils and shake the last bits of fatigue from his mind.

Cole asked, "What about the guys that ran?"

Carl shook his head. "Fucking Customs idiots. I told them to keep it quiet."

"They get away?"

Carl turned, looking at Tony first, then scowled for a moment. "We're looking for them."

Tony cleared his throat in such a way to tell Cole not to press the issue.

Carl relaxed his stare. "Either of you hungry?"

Not waiting for either of them to reply, he told them to give him a bit then meet at the Bagel Café a few blocks up the road. Before they could reply, Carl was walking at a brisk pace back down to the wharf.

"Good or bad?" Cole asked.

Tony laughed, "He's no good, but he's also a detective."

The three of them sat at a corner booth in the Bagel Café, its dark red walls absorbing and erasing the morning light that snuck through in scattered bits from the outside. Carl was intermittently staring at Cole, most certainly trying to figure him out. Tony perused the menu while Cole took turns looking back at Carl when the opportunity arose. He stared for a few long seconds as Carl fidgeted with an inside pocket of his thick winter jacket, which he still wore despite the radiating heat in the small café.

When he finally put both his arms out on the table, Cole thought he saw, at least for a moment, Carl's fingers shaking.

Casually, Tony asked, "What's good?"

"Anything," Carl replied laconically.

Gruff was the right word. Carl hadn't shaved, more than likely for the past two days. His face was that of a fisherman, leathered and stretched tight around his skull. His cheeks and nose were red from the cold, his short-cropped hair a brown leaning more and more towards grey. Knobby fingers steadied themselves on the table as Carl fidgeted again. *Something is off*, Cole thought.

The waitress made her rounds and filled their cups with coffee. Carl wrapped his fingers around her closest leg, just above her knee, and pulled her off-balance against him for a moment before he laughed and let go. She was clearly uncomfortable and tried her best to pretend he hadn't grabbed her. Carl sat back and ordered eggs and bacon, Tony went for an omelet, and Cole went all in for the French toast, looking intently at the uncertainty of her expression. Carl followed up by asking for a glass of orange juice and tried again to grab her, but she shifted to her right and his hand missed. With their orders, she disappeared, leaving the three of them alone, the restaurant just now starting to get some early morning traffic.

Tony ignored Carl's antics and asked, "So, the two guys that ran?"

"Not important," Carl cut him off and continued, "We got the boat, that was five kilos of coke."

"A lot for up here?" Tony asked.

Carl took a sip from his black coffee, "Yeah. That's headline news all over Canada tonight."

The waitress returned with a glass of orange juice and Carl took a long sip, until it was down to two-thirds full. He held it between his hands. Tony looked back to Cole and winked, "This stuff must follow you."

Carl looked at them both, his eyes revealing an immediate displeasure at not understanding the reference.

Tony smiled, "Cole's done a lot of work for the U.S. down in Central America."

Cole grit his teeth, looking first to Carl, then back at Tony. He took a breath, a sip from his coffee, and thought before replying, "For once, this one had nothing to do with me."

Carl, his eyes still piercing in their stare, asked, "So, tell me again. What exactly were you doing up in the middle of the night?"

"Looking at the stars, I guess. You'll have to trust me on that one, Carl."

Cole looked back across the table and fixated on Carl's glass. It was now full again. When he looked up, Carl was staring at him. Cole returned the stare for a few seconds more, both of them sizing the other up. For a moment, he felt the urge to fight him right there in the restaurant.

Carl turned to Tony, "The governor asked me not to meddle in your business."

Tony smiled, "And you said?"

"...that I would."

With that, their food arrived and the three of them dug in, Tony and Carl taking turns to try and see what the other was up to. They spoke little until the food on their plates dwindled to crumbs. Tony was finishing up the last of his meal when he re-entered the conversation.

"I'm not doing anything you wouldn't approve of, Carl. In fact, I'd bet there'll be times we can help you out, like today. I'm here at the request of the governor, simple as that. And he has been more than willing to let us help."

Carl took a long breath, the food having calmed his nerves. He took one last draining sip from his orange juice, then finished off his coffee. They settled their bills with cash and worked their way towards the front door. As Carl and Tony stood in the dusty light of the front door, Cole doubled back. "Forgot a tip. Hang on a second."

He returned around the corner to their table and picked up Carl's glass, raising it to his nose. *Vodka.* He smiled and laughed to himself. It explained much of Carl's mood that morning. He walked quickly back and met the two of them outside, extending his hand to Carl. They shook and Cole nodded, "We'll be seeing ya, Carl."

"Likewise," Carl replied, with his almost ever-present doubtful stare. He started off back towards the docks, leaving Tony and Cole standing on the ice-crusted sidewalk. Since the previous night, the snow had been shoveled mostly off the road and piled nearly a foot tall against each curb. Cars were beginning to line most of the parking spots on both sides of the road and the morning foot traffic had begun to pick up.

Cole asked, "What's today?"

Tony, confused, replied, "What do you mean?"

"What day is it?"

"Tuesday, Cole. It's Tuesday."

With that, they turned for Tony's truck. Cole slept until midday and milled about the living room for some time. Just after noon, he couldn't avoid the sun any longer. It was the first good weather since the onset of winter months ago. The air was still and the sky was a crisp bitter shade of dark blue. Both sides of the entrance to the harbor were blanketed in lines of white, with dark streaks of ancient rock protruding from the steepest lines. He'd stared at it long enough.

"I'm taking a walk."

He didn't need to say any more. Since landing in St. John's, Cole had returned to his old routine of long lonely walks to tire himself out and think of anything other than what was on his mind. Now more than ever, Isabella and Marie were still heavy on his mind, but he knew the stinging pain would subside with time and leave the damn familiar dull ache deep in his gut. That pain was far more manageable.

With his boots, a pair of jeans, and the thick Canada Goose jacket he'd bought in his first week on the island, Cole set out. The North Head trail was closed for the season, but no one seemed to care. It started, oddly enough, at someone's private deck and led around the lower perimeter of the north cliffs. During the summer, it was a busy route, taking most hikers the better part of an hour or more to reach Signal Hill. On days like today, Cole figured there may be a handful of other wandering souls out and about, but more than likely it would afford him some time by himself.

He walked down a few streets then east to the trailhead. It was mostly gravel, occasionally framed by some wooden steps at the steepest sections. As the trail narrowed and wandered its way towards the mouth of the bay, it was increasingly coated in an icy slush that required firm footing. At its most precarious turn, a chain railing had been drilled into the vertical face to help traverse the 20 or so yards where the trail was no more than a foot in width. Just to his right was a near vertical drop nearly 100 feet to the rocks and water below.

Here Cole paused for a moment to take in the sights. To the east, the North Atlantic was once again blanketed by a sea of fog. It was thick and menacing, held back from the land by the relatively warm rocks bathed in sunlight. It hung low and stationary, as if in waiting for an opportunity to roll back in and envelop the land. Above him the sky was a brilliant shade of blue, the sun casting a blinding white light as it started its afternoon run westward. Below him, the water was dark and clear, as a light swell moved in rhythmically, pushing and pulling at the thick seaweed that clung against the rocks. He closed his eyes and listened for some time, feeling a smile slowly take hold.

Moving forward again, Cole reached with his left hand towards the chain and searched for good footing as he stepped over and beside knee-high rocks. On a large flat black stone, he stepped with his right foot and reached forward for the chain as he stepped up and over. His foot flew sideways, towards the water and Cole felt himself falling. Instinct alone thrust his left hand ahead and he caught the chain with four fingers, all his strength now focused on that hand that held him from falling to the water below. With his left foot, he found a patch of gravel as he swung his right hand around to grab at the rock he'd slipped from.

It wasn't the rock, but rather the compacted snow under his boot that had done him in. He pulled himself up further until he was back on solid ground and dusted himself off. Other than a streak of dirty wet snow down the outside of his pant leg from where he'd fallen, he was fine. He turned and looked down to the water and licked his lips, as they'd gone completely dry. Wiping at his pants again, he cursed under his breath, *Fuck*. Looking ahead, he could see that the trail was much improved ahead and he knew that his stubbornness wouldn't let him turn around either way, so he pressed on.

With the icy steps, it took him longer than usual to wrap around the hill and make his way up to the top. Once there, he found the parking lot full as locals and visitors alike were taking in the view. Looking back down, Cole was happy to see that he was the only one who'd come up from the lower trails.

He made his way further back from the crowds to the old stone ruins of what had, at some point in past centuries, been a pub and barracks of some sort. He sat by himself on a dry patch of stone wall for a while longer and caught his breath. Gnarled fingers of the fog bank rolled and twisted against the cliffs below, affording momentary glimpses of the water below. With the fog standing up against itself on one side and the cliffs on the other, no sunlight could reach the shoreline below and the water was a far more ominous shade of blue. He loved this island.

Cole waited until his body had cooled and he felt the first chills against the back of his neck. He was happy he'd taken the North Head trail, but opted to walk the road back down to town. Taking the trail up was risky, but going back down would have been just plain dumb. He dug his hands deep into his pockets, pulled a wool cap low over his head, and walked a quick pace back down by himself, taking one last look at Cabot Tower, perched high above and behind him, a flag hanging limp in the frigid afternoon air. He wondered why it had taken so long to work up the thirst for a beer.

CHAPTER 3: THE SCENE

GREEN SLEEVES WAS slowly building some midweek momentum. Cole had been there, seated at the bar, for two hours, chatting a bit with the bartender. He watched as the first musician of the night set up on the small stage, a low wooden railing around it to keep the hordes from getting too close. The early performers were the up and comers, still hungry for the chance to play for the large and rowdy midnight crowds. Cole didn't recognize the ragged figure on stage and turned back towards his pint of Murphy's. The late afternoon saw a few stragglers come in for beers after work, but the place as a whole lacked the energy that would blossom as the night wore on.

Even with the light from the setting sun outside, the bar's walls, tables, chairs, and even the worn bare floor carried a dark theme. If there were drinking establishments in Newfoundland with brighter tones, Cole had yet to find them. The houses downtown were often brightly painted, but the bars embraced the dark and dreary persona of a long winter season. No matter the time of the day, there was a bar in St. John's that would fool anyone into thinking it was the middle of the night. More than likely, Cole thought, this was a deliberate byproduct of their primary function—a place where one could just as easily hide alone or laugh away an evening with friends. Cole found himself most often opting for the former. He ordered another beer and ran his hand along the length of the wooden bar top. He thought back to his fall earlier that day. If the fall hadn't killed him, the water coupled with a few broken bones surely would have. He thought further back to Harley and his sage advice on pushing one's limits.

Finishing the last sips of his warm beer, he wrapped his hand around the new frosty pint just as soon as the bartender set it in front of him. A moment later, he heard the familiar pop and static of a guitar coming alive through the PA. He turned and watched as the young guy on stage stomped on some of his pedals, adjusted his mic one more time and strummed a few open chords on his mahogany-topped six-string. Its deep and earthy presence echoed throughout the bar as the guy playing began tapping his foot, and he opened up with some American rock and roll. Cole took a long breath and softly nodded along. The music had become one of his favorite ways to pass the seemingly endless winter nights. It would continue into early morning from the dozen or so bars that lined George Street and the surrounding dirty streets.

By the second set, the bar was beginning to fill in. The nameless guy on stage bobbed and weaved like a boxer, stepping back from the mic in between verses before sliding back up and attacking the mic in the next round. He was good, no doubt steadily climbing the ranks of George Street's music scene. After the second set, Cole settled his tab and moved on, further down the narrow and slightly winding street, then down one more block to Water Street. Shamrock City was next on his list and on the far side of the bar, in a corner, he took a seat. Two stools further down, a guy also his age, turned and nodded. Cole recognized him and nodded back, then mouthed the words *Murphy's* to the bartender. She nodded and Cole turned towards Ryan.

"You playing?"

Ryan nodded. "Yeah, in a few. You sticking around?"

"Yeah, for a bit."

"I keep seeing you around. You move up here from somewhere else?"

Cole smiled. "Yeah; came up from the States."

"Working?"

Cole tilted his head, unsure of what to say. "Not exactly, but maybe eventually." He continued, "You're Ryan, right?" Extending his hand, the two shook. "I'm Cole, nice to meet you."

"Good to meet you too, Cole."

Ryan had a glass of whiskey in one hand and he played slowly with his phone in the other, occasionally checking it and setting it back down.

"You're from here?"

Ryan nodded and took a long sip, nearly finishing it before he looked up at the clock. The bartender pushed a pint towards Cole and Ryan, his mouth still full, rattled the ice in his cup, smiled a sly grin, and swallowed. Turning to Cole, he held the grin.

Cole asked, "Loosening up?"

Ryan nodded, replying to himself mostly. "Whatever it takes."

"That shit makes me crazy."

"What shit?"

Cole smiled this time. "Whiskey."

Ryan laughed. "It has that effect on people."

With a topped-off whiskey, he stood up and tipped his glass against Cole's, and then headed for the stage. The sound guy made his way over to the small booth by the wall and Ryan went to work, strumming a bit and fidgeting like everyone seemed to do with their mic before beginning a set. Seconds later, he was playing something Cole didn't recognize. His voice carried across the room, a folksy, almost Americana and raspy sound nearly synced to his battle-worn and spruce-topped guitar. As the night wore on, the music up and down George Street progressively got better and better, until the last few hours before midnight when the energy and the excitement of George Street would peak and explode. It rivaled some of the best cities in the lower 48. Holding onto that thought, Cole felt a good healthy buzz by now.

The bar was filling in with a younger crowd. A far table had what was most certainly an American military air crew. Their short hair and near-constant scanning of the bar gave them away. They were fixated on a table near them that was crowded with half a dozen girls most likely from the nursing school that had made St. John's so famous among the visiting military crews. Cole smiled a bit to himself. If he stuck around, it would likely be an entertaining evening.

He would have stuck around had his spirits been better, but on this particular evening they were not, and so Cole had moved on again after Ryan's first set. As he walked back along Water Street, he held in his mind the chorus of a good drinking song and walked quickly against the frigid wind that had kicked up. It lifted fine particles of frost from the ground and hurled the frozen blinding mist around in mini cyclones along the length of the street, like dust across an open plain. Streetlights cast a pale yellow hue over the soiled and salted snow that littered the ground.

Minutes later, he ducked inside YellowBelly again, walked quickly around the bar, to the stairs, then down into the darkness of the Under-Belly. Around a stone corner, he smiled when he saw her, otherwise keeping his thoughts to himself. Sitting down at his usual spot, the bar was half full, and the tables around it were packed with friends and lovers eating late dinners before the witching hour neared. She smiled at him for a second from the other end of the bar as Cole settled onto his seat.

"Hey Cole."

"Olivia, how are you?"

"Good." She paused for a second, looking at him with some kind of curiosity hidden behind her dark eyes, and continued, "Stout, I assume?"

Cole smiled and nodded. "Please."

A minute later she returned, set the beer down in front of Cole, and studied the quality of her pour for a second or two before leaning against the counter and looking directly at him. She was tall and thin, with dark hair that curled just a bit at her shoulders. Staff at both the YellowBelly upstairs and the UnderBelly downstairs wore plain black outfits, but Olivia seemed to take pride in making the color work for her, and she dressed exceptionally well. Her skin was light against the shadows, and Cole swore that her hair was a different shade of deep red, or brown, or black each time he saw her. It was her lipstick of all things that always seemed to catch his attention, as she never seemed to wear the same color more than once.

Tonight it was blood red, as if she'd just devoured a young unsuspecting man and his innocent crush, and her long lips matched his mood perfectly. Had she worn something lighter, it may very well have lifted his spirits, but he wanted nothing more at that moment than to embrace his sour emotions. He smiled. She laughed.

"What are you smiling about?"

Cole, feeling foolish for a moment, replied, "Nothing really, just enjoying a drink."

He turned the conversation to her. "What've you been up to?"

"Working," she replied with a smirk. She was a happy person, at least from what Cole could surmise, but she rarely let a smile linger on her face for much longer than the fleeting thought that had teased it out of her.

"Did you get out today at all?"

"Lunch with some friends, that was about it. How about you?"

"Went for a walk up to Signal Hill and back earlier."

He thought again to the slip as he took the first long sip from his beer and set the glass back down. Olivia looked over her shoulder at the other patrons then quickly back at Cole, her hair rolling in front of one side of her face. She then reached up, her fingers and hand partly obscured by the long slender sleeve from her shirt, and tucked the strands back behind her ear. Little movements like that were the ones that Cole's mind would hang on to. He was lost for a moment as he tried not to stare for too long. She was beautiful, and Cole enjoyed her company.

"Did you get to see your daughter?"

Cole felt his face freeze for a moment and he fought hard to regain a relaxed composure. He'd forgotten that they'd talked before Isabella and Marie had visited. His mouth was all of a sudden dry, and he tried even harder to not let it show, but she'd already caught onto it.

"Sorry," she said apologetically. "Is everything all right?"

"Yeah, no, it's fine. I did, they came over for a few days."

"I'm sorry. I didn't mean to be rude."

Cole shook his head. "No, no, it's fine. It was good."

Olivia wasn't buying it. With an outstretched hand, she placed her palm on top of his hand. "I'll be back in a second."

Why she'd done that, he wasn't sure, but all at once he wished she'd come back and do it again. Cole clenched his fist then extended his fingers a few times. He watched her as she took an order and went to work behind the bar. Sitting quietly, he watched her spin and reach for bottles to mix up something with whiskey. From his seat, his eyes were drawn to the little bit of momentary space between the tops of her boots and the bottom of her flowing dress. Slivers of her thigh revealed themselves as flashes of pale light as she stepped and twisted behind the bar. *Dammit if she ain't pretty,* he thought.

She returned quickly and asked, "So how long are you staying?"

"Dunno," he said with genuine uncertainty.

"Seems if I made it through the winter, I might as well stay for the summer."

She nodded. "It's gorgeous."

"It's gorgeous right now."

Her head tilted just a bit. "What's gorgeous?"

Cole paused for a second as he'd nearly showed his cards and told her that she was the focus of his comment. "The winter, here. I like it. The snow on the cliffs, the ocean, this town, I like all of it."

"Me, too. Can't imagine living anywhere else."

She looked back once at the rest of the bar, then turned to Cole again and leaned in.

"Can we get some coffee or something tomorrow?"

Cole hadn't expected that, and he fought to constrict his lifted spirits. "Yeah, for sure. Where?"

"A place called Fixed Coffee, just up the road. I usually swing by there on my way to work, maybe around three?"

"Yeah, definitely."

"Cool. So what are you gonna do if you stay?"

"I really don't know. I'm living with a buddy right now, over by the Battery."

She showed some interest. "Not a bad place to spend a winter. Have you been on the trail yet?"

"Yeah, I walked it today."

Her eyes narrowed a bit more than their usual thoughtful gaze. "Icy?"

Cole laughed. "Yeah. Maybe ought to wait a few more weeks."

Before she could answer, a rowdy group of half a dozen entered and called her out by name, with smiles and laughter. She looked at Cole quickly and he nodded, knowing all too well that their shared time for the evening had ended. She hurried over and hugged a few of them, then promptly went to work mixing drinks. Combined with the rest of the crowd that had scampered in to avoid the cold, Cole felt himself drowned out and made his way back outside.

A full band had taken the stage back at Green Sleeves, and Cole nudged his way back in and up to the bar. He felt the eyes of several older women on him and turned to face two of them, standing only a foot or two away. They smiled, and one offered to buy him a shot. Not turning it down, the three of them made small talk for some time over the noise and heat of the packed dance floor. The tables had all been moved back and the entire bar seemed to sway and spin with the crowd. The women drank whiskey, which meant so did Cole, and he could feel the mischievous swirl and burn of one too many shots in his gut.

It wasn't long before he danced with the prettier of the two, spinning her around with force. She was seemingly convinced that she'd hooked him for the night, but Cole was still not in the mood and he focused in on their game of cat of mouse. She tried to lean in, he shifted, then the drunken ballet continued for some time. At some point they'd both lost interest in him, and Cole tooled around the dance floor a few more times with the least timid of the wallflowers. Above the pulsing music, he smiled when he heard them giggle or laugh as he spun them around. He had more drinks, unsure of where they came from, until the midnight hour had long passed. The energy had peaked and would stay that way for some time, until the bars pushed everyone out a few hours before the dawn. The raucous crowd was plenty drunk, and for the most part the mood was light while the band played hard and fast with a guitar, a fiddle, and small drum kit. Cole returned to the bar and as the room seemed to morph and spin, he focused on the music, hearing little more than the steady backbeat.

A finger nudged his chest and he turned to see a small-framed man, likely a few years older the Cole, yelling something at him. He wore ragged green pants and a sweater in desperate need of a cleaning. Unsure, Cole smiled dismissively, which only further aggravated the guy. He was smaller than Cole, but under a thick reddish-blond beard, Cole saw a hardened, angry face. The man yelled again, and Cole shook his head, trying in earnest to understand. The man pushed his finger against his chest once more. Cole leaned into it to avoid being pushed back.

With a thick Newfie accent, all Cole could catch was the twice-repeated "fuck you" and a random sampling of meaningless words, but it became clear that Cole was not liked by his new companion. It didn't help that the guy was clearly drunk, leaning slightly from side to side as he berated Cole. The bartender came over and told the guy to shut up or leave, or something to that effect, but the man persisted.

Cole, still mostly amused, asked, in a fairly friendly manner, "What is it, dude?"

"Fuck you," the guy repeated and went to push Cole again, but Cole blocked his hand and pushed it to the side.

"Fuck you, you don't…" The guy's drunken accent drifted off and Cole missed the second part of his statement, or question, or whatever was the intended point.

The man stepped up closer and spoke now in a deeper and more clear tone, "You fuck off or I'll beat ya down."

He continued, "Fuck you, and you're not from here, so fucking leave. I'll beat ya."

Cole smiled. "I don't think you could beat yourself out of a wet paper bag."

Mischief took over, and Cole's sour mood wasn't helping. He had half a beer left and gulped it down. The bartender looked over and Cole nodded to assure him that all was calm, but it clearly wasn't.

"I'll fucking beat ya." As he said it, the guy drifted just a bit to his side and caught the bar with his hand. There was anger in his piercing eyes, but Cole guessed that he was just drunk and pissed at an American dancing with the local talent. Nevertheless, he hadn't been in a fight for some time.

Cole nodded towards the side door. "Let's go then."

He followed the drunk outside and as he turned slightly right, the man took a swing at him. Cole stepped back, looking over his shoulder at the camera on the street light where the alley met George Street.

"Not here, further up." Cole motioned with his flattened palm and walked casually a bit further up the alley. Unbelievably, the guy followed him, muttering curses under his breath. Once out of sight from the camera, Cole turned, smiled, and spoke plainly, "All right; go ahead, bud."

Cole dodged the first punch, the cold air filling his lungs as he felt the slow onset of adrenaline. He hadn't felt that in months, since leaving Cozumel. The guy lunged again and grabbed Cole's sleeve for a second before Cole circled his hand back to break the drunk's grip. He punched, and one more time again before Cole threw his first punch that landed solidly against the guy's cheek. It didn't seem to dissuade him from continuing the fight. The drunk lunged at Cole and grabbed at his shirt again, twisting Cole a bit to a point where he was surprised by the drunk's strength. Even with that, Cole was able to free himself once more and steady his footing.

The guy swung wildly and when he did, Cole connected a second time, this time on his mouth, and a steady stream of blood blew out onto the snow as he exhaled. The guy wiped at his lip, looked for a moment at the blood now covering his hand, and pulled a straight-bladed knife from somewhere under his oversized wool sweater. He gripped it tight while staring at Cole.

Sobering up quickly and licking his lips, Cole knew the fun was now over. As the drunk lunged at him again, Cole stepped back, but the man moved forward to counter it and lunged again. Twice more, Cole moved back until he was out of room before the drunk lunged again and swung wide, missing his target. Cole grabbed hold of the arm wielding the knife and pressed it against the wall, but the man shook loose with a renewed violence. Cole held firm, but at some point, he felt the blade through his sleeve as it caught some flesh on his right arm.

Cole steadied his nerves and was able to press the drunk into the wall before throwing some elbows into the back of his neck. The drunk spun free once more, but Cole surged and body-checked him again into the wall, both of them facing each other now with Cole barely holding a grip on the man's sleeve. The man tried to punch, but couldn't get a good start with his back against the wall. Cole, on the other hand, threw more elbows at the man's face and when he tried to block them, Cole grabbed onto his collar and threw his knee several times into his torso. Cole was gaining the advantage.

The drunk turned his face towards the wall to avoid another blow to his face, and Cole seized a fistful of collar behind the man's neck with his left hand and paused. He hoped, for a brief moment, that perhaps the drunk would come to his senses, but he didn't, and he squirmed to free his knife hand. Cole didn't hesitate to throw a hard knee up and into the side of the drunk's skull. His head against the wall, Cole felt the crunch when his knee struck, and he instinctively held the guy for a few seconds more until he fell limp to the ground. The snow and slush was stained with dirt and blood, both of their footsteps having soiled what had been an undisturbed and pretty plain of white in a back alley. Cole wiped his face and took steady breaths to regain his composure. His forearm burned, and he felt at the small gash in his jacket. His finger against the skin where he was cut, he knew in a quick moment that it was nothing more than an inconvenience. He'd won.

The drunk was flat on the ground, motionless, and laying contorted on his side. Blood still trickled out from his busted lip, but otherwise he didn't look to be in too bad of shape. Cole recalled the crunch and feared that he'd done far more damage than what was visible to the naked eye. He walked down to George Street, not more than 25 yards away, and looked up and down the now crowded street. It was nearing the end of the night, and this was the time when folks young and old latched on to someone to take home for the evening. Some stumbled side to side, others seemed slightly more composed, but the street practically stunk of beer, whiskey, and hot dogs from the street vendors.

Cole found a girl, standing outside the deck of Green Sleeves, seemingly waiting for her friends. "Can you go tell that ambulance down there that a guy is passed out in the alley?"

She looked at him funny. "Huh?"

Cole exhaled, frustrated, and repeated himself, "Go tell that ambulance there's a guy in the alley. He looks beat up."

She stared at him as if she didn't comprehend.

"Please?"

Dismissively, she mouthed, "OK."

As she started walking, Cole crossed the street, then walked further to the end of George Street until he was nearly out of sight. He watched the girl get the attention of the driver, then continued to watch from a distance as the ambulance pulled up and both paramedics stepped out and walked up the alley. With that, Cole turned and walked alone back to Tony's.

CHAPTER 4: OLD HABITS

HE WOKE UP in his bed this time, the room dark except for the yellow light that snuck in from under the door. Tony was up and moving around, the rhythm of his steps and the smell of bacon telling Cole that breakfast was out there, if only he could bring himself to get up. As he contemplated making his first movements of the day, Tony called out rather loudly for him. That was soon followed by frustrated footsteps nearing the door. Seconds later, the door shook with three thuds from Tony's fist and then he pushed it open.

"Cole."

"Huh," He mumbled from under the sheets.

"Cole, get up."

"But Dad…"

"Dammit, Cole, I'm not kidding. Get up. I'm assuming the bloody towel in the sink is yours."

Tony had Cole's interest now and he moved slowly from one side, to his back, then to the other before he rolled and sat up. A dish towel was wrapped around his right forearm and cinched tight with two zip-ties. He recognized them as the green ones from the kitchen drawer, where Tony kept some random supplies. Cole had jokingly called it the *spy drawer*: an eclectic mix of knives, flashlights, duct tape, zip-ties, batteries, and random tools.

Standing up and pulling a shirt over his head, he walked slowly out of his room, towards the kitchen, and squinted at the mid-morning light. Tony had poured him a cup of coffee, and Cole appreciated the kindness of the act despite his present condition. He sat down and took a slow sip.

"What the hell did you do?"

Cole looked at Tony for a moment, thinking that if he could immediately recall all of the details, he would. But he could only remember dancing.

With a fake Arkansas drawl, Cole spoke slowly, "I did not have sexual relations with that woman."

Tony almost laughed, but he didn't, which frustrated Cole. "What's with the bloody towel?"

"Dunno."

"And the balled up roll of Duct Tape?"

Cole just shook his head. *Nothing*, he thought.

"There's blood on the floor, too."

With that, Cole remembered the fight, first in bits and pieces. He thought hard about the drunk fisherman and recalled with some clarity the guy's persistence. The image that came to mind was the fresh crimson-stained snow from the alley and the look on his face after Cole had busted his lip. That thought brought him to the knife, but the details beyond the image of it in the drunken man's hand were too far gone in a whiskey haze.

"I might have gotten in a fight."

"Did you lose?"

Cole squinted at Tony, not missing the subtle jab. "No, I don't think so."

"You don't think so, or you don't remember?"

"I didn't lose," Cole said as he turned to look out across the room and towards the water. It was another calm day, albeit with overcast skies. The snow-crusted cliffs on either side of the harbor painted the more familiar and foreboding scene that he'd come to appreciate over the long winter. In a lot of ways, he was glad to see the darkness.

Tony brought over a plate of eggs and bacon, "Let me see your arm."

Cole's head was still dazed from the night before, but he didn't feel nearly as bad as he expected. With his left arm holding a fork, he took a few bites while Tony lifted up his bad arm.

"Ahhhhh, that fucking hurts."

Tony was trying to cut the zip-ties that cinched the towel around his arm.

"I'm assuming you were too drunk to manage the intricacies of Duct Tape."

"That sounds about right," Cole said with his first smile of the day.

Tony removed both of them and let the towel drop to the table. Cole lifted his arm to get the first quasi-sober look at the cut. It was a few inches, and not all that deep, but had made quite a mess.

"You're cleaning this shit up, I hope you know that."

Cole said nothing and reached for his coffee. Tony stood up and went over to the cabinets by the sink, pulling down a medium-sized bag, and then set it back down on the kitchen counter. In no time, he'd doused Cole's arm in iodine and affixed three butterfly bandages, evenly spaced along the length of the cut.

"Where'd you learn all that?"

Tony shook his head. "It ain't that complicated."

Cole finished his cup and set it down, taking a long breath, and looking out across the room.

"What are you doing here, Tony?"

"What do you mean?"

"I mean, what is this? What are we doing here?"

"Well, I can tell you we're not here to get in bar fights."

Cole laughed. "Yeah, I figured as much." He paused, took a long breath then continued. "Sorry."

Tony was cleaning up the packaging from the iodine and bandages. Cole's question was clearly still on his mind.

"Clean up this shit, and wipe the blood up off the floor in the kitchen. Then we'll talk."

Noon came and went. Cole cleaned up the spots of blood off the wooden floor, which he found slightly amusing as they indicated he'd walked around the entirety of the kitchen and living room with no clear purpose or direction. From out of the sink, he tossed the towel and balled-up rolls of Duct Tape. How he couldn't remember any of it was beyond him. His head was heavy, but still he felt better than he thought appropriate given the evidence of a bender scattered randomly about the house.

Tony emerged some time later from upstairs. Cole didn't bother him when he was up there. He knew there were two rooms, one where Tony slept and the other served as an office or study perhaps, the door always closed. Downstairs, he grabbed a beer from the fridge and offered one to Cole, but he declined and opted for water to bring some life back to his sandpaper tongue.

They both sat at the couches by the big windows overlooking the channel. Cole said nothing, waiting patiently to see what Tony had to say. A full minute went by before Cole couldn't stand it any longer.

"Did Johnson send you here?"

Tony smiled a bit, shaking his head softly. "You don't mince words, do you?"

"Was it Panama?"

Tony looked straight at him, expressionless. "Yeah, it was Panama."

Cole had known deep down that was likely the case, but this was the first time Tony had validated his thoughts. He despised the idea of any more guilt. At times, it hung from his neck like a chain that worked against his every movement. Frustrated, he spoke too soon.

"So am I a charity case now?"

"Cole."

"Seriously, what are we doing here? What are you doing here?"

He was mad now, even more mad at himself for lashing out at Tony, who had by all accounts saved his life in Panama.

"It's a post, Cole, just like any other. It may not be where I want to be, but I'll do it for as long as they want me to. And I'll do this as well as I can."

"Who is they?"

Tony smiled. It was remarkable how calm he could be in the tensest of situations. Cole had seen Tony's impeccable character on the streets of Key West, in Nicaragua with armed soldiers, and now in a remote outpost in the northernmost reaches of North America.

"Who do you think, Cole?"

"I stopped asking that question a long time ago."

"Similar task force, just like Panama. This is just another front in the same quiet war." Tony turned the conversation towards Cole. "Speaking of Johnson, what ever happened in Cozumel?"

It was Cole's turn to play the game, and he sat back against the cushions on the couch and thought back to that night speeding down a dark gravel road. He thought first of the island, the evening breeze, and the pastel colors of their villa. His mind then wandered to Claire, then to Matt, and finally to Harley. Once there, he snapped himself quickly out of that dark pit, and back to the drive with Johnson.

"Dunno, I never saw him."

Tony took a long breath before speaking. "By the time I saw the report, half the damn thing was blacked out."

They both sat in silence for a while longer. Cole finished his glass of water and set the cup in front of him on a table. He crossed his legs and felt at the cut on his arm, now increasingly confident that it would heal in a few days at most.

He asked, "Does this bother you?"

Tony replied, "Does what bother me?"

"Being here?"

"No, why would it?"

Cole shrugged, "It just seems a little quiet for you."

"I've been doing this for a while, Cole. With time, you sometimes hope for the quiet jobs, the assignments that might give you a bit of a break." He paused for a moment, thinking carefully about his words. "Sometimes it ain't a bad thing to take a bit of time to recover. Our time will come to jump back into the fray."

Cole knew that Tony rarely went into much detail unless the need arose. His concise words were as much insight as Cole could have hoped for and, despite the lack of specifics, it was enough context for Cole to sit back and think for a few moments.

He asked, "And me?"

Tony grinned, showing a genuine appreciation for Cole and all of his imperfections. "I figure you could use a break just as much as me."

Cole sank further back and thought on the meaning of a break. It seemed a foreign concept to him, an idea his mind had long ago forgot to even consider.

Tony asked, "You doing anything today?"

"Going out for coffee."

Tony's gaze shifted and he focused on Cole's face, looking for some glimmer of a detail. He spared no time and cut right to the question at hand. "With who?"

Cole cleared his throat, "A Girl."

"Olivia?"

Fuck, Cole thought. *I say too damn much.* He immediately regretted having told Tony about her, about the way he'd been caught by her looks and her quiet subtle mood shifts from behind the bar. Looking away, he pretended to be consumed by something out on the water.

"Good for you," Tony said.

"It's nothing. We're just meeting up for a bit."

"No, I mean it, Cole. It's good."

He laughed to himself, embarrassed as if he was a grade-school kid caught putting cologne on before a Friday night school gymnasium dance.

"I should get going," he said decisively as Tony made no attempt to hide the smile on his face.

Cole walked towards the door, reaching for his jacket. "Seriously, it's nothing."

As he opened the front door, Tony called out, "Behave."

"See ya, Tony."

He was early to the coffee shop, half an hour before Olivia had suggested they meet up. As he walked past the front windows, he was caught off guard when she looked right at him from a stool inside. A glare against the window, she tilted her head and smiled, which only worsened his footing, and for a moment Cole worried he might fall down right there on the sidewalk in front of her.

Re-caging his emotional compass, he walked inside to the counter, smiled towards Olivia, and ordered a cup of their darkest roast. While he waited, he found himself unsure of what to do. He could go talk to her or wait for his coffee. Neither seemed ideal, so he stood there awkwardly for a minute or two more until the server brought his mug. He dropped in two cubes of sugar, not caring the least about stirring it, and walked as casually as he could over to Olivia.

She wore a pair of jeans, the denim painted on along her long thighs and a dark shirt that hung low over her waist, the sleeves opening up wide at her wrists. Her hair seemed lighter, although it was most likely the abundance of light in the small cafe and nothing more. She turned towards him, smiling, and offered a casual, "Hey there."

Cole was drawn in to her cherry-red lipstick and had it not been for the movement of her lips, he might have missed her words entirely. As was so often the case, his mood lightened with the brighter shade she'd chosen for the night.

"Hi." He could think of nothing else to say.

A moment passed before he put every ounce of energy into thinking of something to kick off the conversation.

"What time are you working?"

She took a sip and set her coffee down, turning back to him. "About an hour or so."

Cole smiled at the thought of her company for an hour.

"You're from here, right?"

She nodded. "Yeah, this is home. What about you?"

Cole thought for a second, "I'm from the States; grew up on the East Coast."

He didn't want to talk about himself, so he quickly followed up, "I like your lipstick."

It was a bit on the audacious side, but she smiled and stumbled for a second with a reply. Cole laughed, and a moment later she did too.

"Sorry," he said. "I know that's a bit random."

"No, no. Thanks, I guess." A partial smile spread across her pretty face. Cole laughed a genuine laugh, too, and she let go of any attempt to hold it in. Her full smile was warm and put him at ease, marking an entry into a comfortable conversation.

"So, besides George Street, what am I missing in St. Johns?"

"For St. John's, that's about it. But when you get out of town, that's where it really shines."

They talked for another half hour or so before she abruptly asked about the time. Cole checked his watch and she seemed flustered for a second. He took that as a good sign, thinking perhaps she'd enjoyed his company as much as he'd enjoyed hers.

"I needed an afternoon like this. Thanks."

She looked at him quizzically, on the verge of digging deeper towards the meaning of such a simple statement.

"Yeah, well, you should come by tonight. First drink is on me."

Cole nodded, "Deal. I'll see ya then."

When they left, Cole walked down the street with her up to the doors of the YellowBelly. She hugged him and he held on tight for a moment, shuddering at the first affection he'd felt in the better part of year. Her hair tickled his nose just as he caught a momentary hint of perfume.

She let go and asked, "Are you OK?"

"Yeah, sorry. Just a bit cold, I guess." He paused. "I'll see ya later."

She turned to walk inside.

Cole stood on the curb, alone with the wind for a few seconds more, unsure of which winding road he'd walk for the next few hours. Up the street and to the left sat the madness of George Street. Straight ahead, he could walk back towards the Battery. A block down, he could meander alone along the wharf. Conflicting emotions pulled him in different directions, and he relished the freedom of no particular pressure either way. In any case, he'd see her again tonight. He opted to walk for a bit, perhaps until the sun went down and the drunken hordes blossomed again under a winter moon on George Street. It was brutally cold, but he felt warm and smiled to himself as he set off down the road.

CHAPTER 5: ALLURE

A LIGHT SNOW hurried along with the gusting winds as the sun dropped below the low and obscured western horizon. Its pale yellow light in between the clouds did nothing to ward off the nighttime chill. Cole walked the length of the wharf, beyond downtown to the working areas of the harbor. A good number of fishing boats were tied two or even three abreast, their captains no doubt impatiently waiting for the weather to turn and show even the slightest hint of spring. With darkness taking hold, Cole reached the end, turned, and walked back towards George Street.

He found a seat at Green Sleeves, took a corner seat, and slowly drank stouts through the first two sets. Ryan was on stage, his hair matted and slick with sweat, and he'd nodded slightly with a smile when Cole walked past. With his guitar strapped across his chest, he glanced at the bar and they traded looks. His options were to take a break or play through, and Cole was curious to see which way he'd go. A moment later, Ryan started playing again, betting that his weathered voice could take advantage of the momentum that had been boiling up on the dance floor. It was a local crowd, and he tailored his songs to their liking, accentuating a defiant Celtic flair in his voice. Cole ordered a third—or perhaps it was a fourth—stout and sat a bit closer to the stage. He strained to catch the words and paid little attention to the swelling masses.

Ryan's set ended, and with a few clicks and the momentary squelch of the speakers, the house music came back on for the brief interlude before the next act took the stage. He ordered his usual whiskey on the rocks and found a seat next to Cole.

"How ya been, Cole?"

"Good. You earned your pay tonight."

Ryan nodded. "Yeah. Good crowd for a weeknight."

Cole asked, "College kids?"

Ryan laughed. "Seems that way, doesn't it?"

"You play anywhere else tonight?"

"Nah, three hours is enough for me. I'm spent. And you?"

Cole looked around at the bar. "Dunno; might stay up a bit tonight."

Ryan drained his whiskey and stood up, patting Cole hard on the shoulder. "Have a good one then. Feels like something's cooking tonight."

With that, he grabbed his guitar case from the corner of the stage and made his way unceremoniously towards the door. The next performer was already plugging in, looking up for a second to take in the packed floor as the congregation swayed and shouted. Cole had been there too long, and he opted to settle his tab and move on.

It was nearing ten in the evening and George Street was awash in people walking randomly about in a dozen different directions. The snow on the street was matted down, melted, and mixed into a dirty brown slush. More still was piled up against the curbs, standing nearly a foot tall and solid, having frozen, thawed, and re-frozen again over the past few days. Girls in short skirts and heels stepped carefully over the snow banks to stand and shiver in entrance lines at the scattered bars and clubs.

Cole walked on, unsure as to where he'd end up. As he did, some young girl broke from her friends, hooked her arm around his, and pulled him towards her posse. They were giggling, laughing, and before he knew it, Cole was nearly in the middle of the five of them.

"Come dance with us," she said with a smile.

Barely 20, she had dark hair and a gorgeous complexion, complete with freckles across her cheeks and nose. *Damnit,* Cole thought.

"Why not?" He asked casually, and she pulled him in closer. He stumbled, realizing that perhaps his count of stouts was off by a few. As a group, they veered to the curb, over the snow bank, and into a short line for Club Allure. Cole had not been inside before, knowing it attracted a younger crowd with unpalatable mix of techno-trance dance music. He huffed low and under his breath as she pulled him through the door, a bouncer offering nothing more than the most subtle of a nod in his direction.

Inside, the walls shook with music ricocheting across all corners of the place. Cole felt it thumping against his brain and regretted his decision. Still she pulled him in close, against her, and yelled, "I'm Chelsea."

He smiled and yelled back, "I'm Cole."

She moved backwards, pulling him along further into the crowd and began to throw her arms and hips from side to side. Whatever they were doing was well was beyond his abilities on a dance floor. The girls spun around and were joined by a notably smaller kid in a tank top who moved with an even more absurd energy than any three other people combined. They were apparently all friends, and Cole slowly moved back and leaned an elbow against the bar.

"Whiskey," he yelled when the young blonde bartender swung by him.

He watched from a distance as the girls moved in and out of the crowd and laughed at the occasional appearance of the kid as he jumped and spun. Cole thought he could see steam coming off the backs of the sweating mass of moving bodies. Chelsea and one of her friends marched over to Cole.

"Come dance," she said to him, practically begging him to join them.

"You want a drink?"

It was clear that neither of them would turn down a free drink, so Cole turned and motioned with three fingers to the bartender, who was in the middle of pouring his shot. She returned moments later with three small glasses and set them down. Cole handed her cash and he passed out the shots to each of them.

"Here's to George Street," Cole toasted, and they each emptied their glasses. The larger of Chelsea's friends pulled at Cole and kissed him. He appreciated the audacity of it and didn't object. Over the roaring music, he could sense the alcohol-induced bliss of their evening. The girls went back to dancing. Cole watched for a few minutes more and then the kid appeared out of nowhere, slowing down until he stopped right next to Cole.

She likes you…" he said.

Half-joking, Cole asked, "Which one?"

"Chelsea."

"She's cute."

"Not your type?"

"She's cute, just caught me off-guard a bit."

The kid rolled his eyes, and it was clear to Cole that the kid was feeling him out. His thin frame was covered in sweat, most of it likely his.

"Do you have a girlfriend?"

Cole shook his head, "Nope."

"Want one?"

Cole shook his head again, knowing that George Street nearing midnight was not the place to fall in love.

"Boyfriend?"

Cole coughed, the question completely catching him off-guard. "Nah, sorry bud. Not my thing."

The kid shrugged. "No problem; just had to try."

Cole laughed out loud and shook his head, and the kid did the same. "I'm Timmy," he said.

Cole was unsure of what to do and in a moment of awkwardness, he extended his hand to shake the kid's.

"What are we, forty?"

Cole laughed again. "Sorry. I'm Cole. It's nice to meet you, dude."

Timmy smiled, looked back at the dance floor, and suddenly leapt back into the madness. Cole replayed the previous few minutes in his head, the thoughts complicated by the endless thumping of some bass rhythm from the DJ up on stage. He watched for details, as he'd learned to do in Cozumel. It was a pulsing, moving, living body of people that threw themselves about in rhythmic waves, a DJ situated at a table on a stage in front of them with his hands punching wildly into the air.

In the middle of it, Cole saw Chelsea and a few of her friends stop on the floor with Timmy. They each took something in their hands, brought them to their mouths, then went back to dancing. Cole was proud of himself for catching the subtle detail of their pill swap, convinced that he hadn't lost his edge during the dormant months since he'd left Mexico. He thought briefly of Matt and Harley, then stopped himself from going any further.

He ordered another round of whiskey, certain that Chelsea's friends wouldn't object. Armed with four shots of the cheapest house whiskey, he proceeded into the mix and found a few of them circling Chelsea in some erotic kind of group dance that bordered on public indecency. They were not the least bit disappointed when he disrupted their gyrations and offered them drinks. They each took shots again and circled close around Cole, pressing themselves against him, his arms high over his head in a moment of emotionally complex social uncertainty. He looked up at the high ceiling overhead and laughed carelessly, caught up in, and enjoying, a moment of madness.

Not long after, he retreated once again towards the bar and leaned up against a wooden railing. The entire space was dark and almost dreary, save for the red, green, and yellow lights that danced in frantic pulsing circles around the walls and rafters. He was more and more convinced that in a former life the place had been a pub, but now had been hastily converted into a nightclub. His ears hurt and he thought it best to get to leaving soon, if not for home then at least for somewhere where the walls didn't tremble so much.

He heard a faint yell, followed by a second, a third, and what quickly turned into a chaotic chorus of screams muted only by the dance music. Perking up and looking around, he saw at least two people laid out on the dance floor. A few tried to help, but most ran off for the back and front doors. In a matter of seconds, the floor had all but cleared. There were two younger guys on the floor, contorted and shak-ing. Each had one or two others trying to hold them still, but they wore expressions on their faces that showed their utter fear and inability to render even the most basic of first aid.

Cole's attention shifted to the door, where he saw Chelsea and her friends trying desperately to get another one of their girlfriends outside. Cole moved quickly towards them, catching up just as they made it out-side the two glass doors and to the curb. The bigger girl who had grabbed him earlier had now fallen down into the snow. She was sprawled over the snow bank, bent at the waist, her head down in the muddied slush. One of her friends tried to hold her head up and Cole could see that her eyes had rolled back deep and she was in some kind of seizure. Chelsea tried to pull her friend's short skirt down to cover her underwear and restore some of the girls' dignity as she laid in the snow.

Cole grabbed Chelsea's arm, "Did you call an ambulance?"

Her eyes were wide open, desperation pouring out unchecked, and she didn't seem to comprehend his words.

He repeated himself, "Ambulance?"

She shook her head. "No."

"Give me your phone," he barked.

He quickly dialed the police and tersely told them to start sending as much as they could towards George Street. He mentioned some-thing about an overdose, then hung up, not feeling the need to elabo-rate. By that point, Chelsea's friend was unresponsive and the girls were howling with increasingly piercing shrieks. He looked up and around at George Street, and the crowd that was now forming around Allure. He caught a quick glimpse of Timmy, over in the shadows. When the two made eye contact, Timmy turned and ran, disappearing into the crowd.

Chelsea was by now hysterical. Cole turned to one of her friends who, while still frantic, seemed to be keeping herself somewhat better composed.

Calmly, he said, "Stay with her. Paramedics are coming."

She nodded softly and held the girl's lifeless head up and out of the snow.

Cole hopped up and took off towards where he'd seen Timmy run. As he made it one block farther, the street was again crowded with young guys and girls spilling out from yet another club. Three more were unconscious and lying in the snow with their friends trying desperately to help. Girls huddled in groups and cried while the young men looked around in disbelief, sobering up quickly the reality of their circumstances.

Cole ran further, another block or two, and caught another glimpse of Timmy, in an alley, arguing with two other men. From George Street, Cole stopped and made eye contact once more. The three of them split up and ran, Cole setting off in the direction that Timmy took. He overtook him a minute later and grabbed at Timmy's shirt. Steam rose off his sweaty shoulders and poured out from his open mouth as he gasped for air. He squirmed to break away from Cole, but was no match for Cole's grip.

Cole asked, "What happened?"

Timmy spun hard to free himself again, but not avail. "Let go!" He screamed.

Cole grabbed tighter and pressed Timmy against a wall. "What happened? Just tell me what happened!"

Timmy kicked at Cole's shin, catching him off guard, and as Cole lifted his leg up and back in pain, Timmy broke free and ran again, farther down the road, where he took a hard left up an alley. Cole hesitated to put weight back down on his leg as he winced and steadied himself with one hand against a cold and wet brick wall.

Fuck, he thought. It wasn't Cole's kind of fight. Timmy, with his small stature and wild dance floor antics, was not the type to throw punches, and over the pain in his leg, Cole smiled and shook his head, wondering for a moment what Harley would have thought of the encounter. Timmy was now gone, and Cole had lost the urge to chase him down again.

He doubled back up towards George Street and stopped in the middle of the street once he saw the unfolding scene. There were half a dozen ambulances, their red and blue lights reflecting off the dark brick and wooden walls of George Street. The puddles of melted snow magnified the chaos of the lights, forcing Cole to squint as he stared. Walking farther, there were police and paramedics moving deliberately around no less than two dozen bodies laid out in the street and on the sidewalks. Much of the screaming had subsided as people seemed to be in the mature stages of shock and disbelief. The first responders were working from one end of George up to the next, and as Cole walked, hobbling on his bad leg and trying to walk off the pain, his mind raced to put the pieces together. He then caught his first glimpse of two bodies under white sheets, all but abandoned as the medics had moved on to others. He struggled to breathe and felt his heart punching against his chest. Those that weren't affected had all fled, leaving only the friends of victims to stand and wonder what to do next. Music still echoed out from one or two bars on opposite ends of George Street, as if the party continued on unaffected by the carnage.

Standing by himself, just above the turn down towards Water Street, Cole stood motionless with the back of YellowBelly behind him. The ambulances and police cars had silenced their sirens, leaving only their flashing lights to keep George Street from going dark. In the distance, more were coming and the faint whine of their sirens carried across what was otherwise an eerie silence on George Street. The music had stopped.

"Cole?"

He turned to see Olivia at the back entrance. He looked at her for a moment, unsure of what to feel, and he slowly walked over to join her.

"What happened?" she asked.

"Dunno. Drugs, I guess. There's bodies up and down George Street."

She put her hand up to her mouth and stared to her left, shaking her head. An unmarked police car came up and around, parking a few yards further down George Street. Carl hopped out from the passenger side and didn't seem to notice Cole or Olivia standing by the wall. Olivia stepped back into a shadow, looking as if she'd seen a ghost. Carl walked slowly towards a group of officers, and they turned to open up their circle to him. They talked casually, a few of them shaking their heads. Carl rubbed at his chin, looking down at the ground, and nodded.

"I should go," Olivia said with a trembling voice.

Cole's attention snapped back to her and he thought to ask about Carl. He reached out and grabbed her hand, pulling slowly. She leaned into his embrace.

"Be careful," he said.

She nodded and turned to walk back inside. She was already frantically texting away on her phone, and Cole surmised that she had very real concerns for some of her own friends.

Well after midnight, Cole limped up the three steps into Tony's house. Tony was sitting in the kitchen, his phone on the table next to him, and looked up when Cole walked in. "What happened?"

Cole blinked, not knowing how to answer. "I dunno. Something hit George Street like a freight train."

"Drugs?" Tony asked.

Cole nodded. "Yeah. I think it was pills."

Tony focused on Cole. "How do you know that?"

"I saw some kids passing them out a minute or two before it all went crazy."

Tony thought for a moment, looked down at his phone, spun it once in his hand, then back to Cole.

"You didn't happen to get any, did you?"

Cole shook his head, "Nah, didn't think to." He paused. "But I saw one kid passing them out. I'd recognize him if I see him again. I chased him, but he got away."

"You're limping."

"Yeah. The kid got me pretty good in the shin."

Tony laughed, then apologized. "Sorry. Not really funny under the circumstances."

Cole laughed, too. "Nah, it's all right. Had me thinking about what Harley would've thought."

After a brief silence, Tony asked, "How bad is it on George Street?"

Cole took a long breath. "It ain't good."

CHAPTER 6: THE GOVERNOR

COLE WOKE THE following morning to some voices in the living room. He laid in his bed for another 20 minutes or so before reluctantly rolling over and pulling on last night's clothes. Out in the living room, two men in suits sat at the couch and turned, nodding to Cole before going back to doing nothing much. In the kitchen, Cole poured himself a cup of coffee and asked the men if they'd like some. They each shook their heads no, uncomfortable with their current surroundings.

Cole asked, "Y'all seen Tony?"

One of them looked upstairs for a moment, then back down at Cole, before ignoring the question.

Cole continued, "Well, I for one am hung-OVER and could use some breakfast. Eggs?"

Now the two men simply looked at each other with stern expressions, offering nothing in reply.

Cole scrambled up some eggs, loaded them with cheddar cheese, scrambled them up some more, and laid the mess of a breakfast out on a plate, walking confidently into the living room and sitting down at a chair by the couch. He slurped at his coffee deliberately to watch for any reaction.

Taking the first big bite from his plate, he asked, "Y'all cops?"

They ignored him, the ensuing awkward silence interrupted briefly when one of them cleared his throat.

Cole wasn't getting anywhere with them. He looked up to the second floor at the closed door and wondered what Tony was up to. For a second, he questioned to himself if it was something bad, but the living room didn't seem to hold that kind of tension. He sat in silence, eating his breakfast for a few minutes more, then returned to the kitchen. As he was washing his dishes, he heard the door upstairs crack open. Down the stairs came yet another older man in a suit, his cheeks unmistakably red with Irish genes. Tony followed behind him. The two men at the couch stood up and buttoned their jackets.

At the door, the older man turned and looked at Cole for a brief moment, then turned to Tony. He asked, "Is that him?"

Tony nodded. "Yes, Sir. That's Cole Williams."

"Does he have a clearance?"

Tony chewed at his lip, tilted his head, and looked to Cole, "Do you?"

Cole finished his coffee and thought for a moment before replying. "Not that I'm aware of."

The governor rubbed at the side of his mouth and nodded softly, "I'll send someone over to work on that."

"Thank you, Sir. Please let me know what we can do."

The party of three left quietly, and Cole watched from the kitchen as they got into a dark sedan and started back up from the Battery and towards town.

Cole finished at the sink and asked, "Who were they?"

Tony was still looking out the window as the car disappeared around a corner. "The governor."

"Is this about last night?"

"Yup."

Cole looked at Tony for any more insight. "What does he want?"

"I don't know just yet."

"We got work to do or something?"

Tony smiled. "You do."

"What?"

Tony walked over, took a seat at the table, and grinned. "You better make a list."

"Of what?"

"All the places you've been for the last ten years. He's gonna try to get you a security clearance so you can get read in on this."

"On what?"

Tony smiled. "Start making that list. People who've known you too."

———————

Cole sat at the living room table well into the afternoon. He listed *Delaney*, Key West, Panama, Key West again, Cozumel, France, Chiswick, and a smattering of random travels, but he found himself staring at the paper in front of him when he thought back to Martinique. Isabella was the only person he'd known there. He listed her again when he wrote out the details of Carentan. It put him squarely into a dark place. With two pages of notes, he rolled onto the couch and stared up at the grey sky through the big living room window.

He slept for some time, waking late in the afternoon in the same place, unsure of where his dreams had taken him in the past hour or so, but his stiff neck told him that his mind had not wandered further than the streets of Carentan, or memories of Isabella, and finally Marie. He did nothing that evening, despite his best efforts to shake himself free of whatever grey cloud had rolled in over him. He tried a few times to get up and go for a walk, never making it further than the front door.

He woke the following morning on the couch again. The absence of booze had given him more solid sleep than he'd had in weeks, if not months. It was early in the morning, some thin lines of purple intermixed with the pale yellow light that marked the beginning of another day. He brewed some coffee and sat silently by himself. The pain had mostly subsided, although the same persistent thoughts hung heavy on his mind. Outside, the air was still, the water in the channel like a sheet of glass that took slow breaths up and down with the small swell that rolled in softly from the east. He grit his teeth, telling himself to get dressed and get moving lest the claws from yesterday sink into him again.

Minutes later, with jeans and a sweatshirt on, he emerged from his room and was met by Tony in the living room.

"Carl's on his way over."

Cole stopped in his tracks, thought for a moment, then turned to Tony. "Why?"

"He wants to talk to you."

"When?"

"Now."

Cole took a long and frustrated breath. He wasn't worried about Carl, but the thought of being stuck in the house for another day pissed him off. The sounds of footsteps at the door broke the silence in the room, and Tony walked over to let him in.

"Coffee?"

Carl nodded, taking a seat at the couch, the normal level of frustration painted on his ruddy face.

"Cole?"

He turned to Tony. "Huh?"

"Coffee?"

"Fuck it. Why not?"

Cole walked over to the other chair and sat down, Carl watching his every movement. Neither spoke until Tony brought over two cups and went back for his own.

Tony asked, "What happened last night?"

Carl's eyes narrowed as he thought over the question. He gruffly replied, "A bunch of kids overdosed."

Tony sat down, taking in the tension between Cole and Carl. He tried his best to calm things down a bit, asking, "Any idea where it came from?"

Carl stared at Cole for a moment more, then turned to Tony, "No, not yet."

He continued, "I was busy working another case." He paused and returned his stare to Cole, before continuing, "You know anything about a local getting his head smashed in off George Street?"

Carl was apparently a better detective than Cole had given him credit for. He almost smiled, but caught himself before his lips curled.

He shook his head, "No." Cole played dumb and tried to steer the conversation back towards the previous night. "Are the two related?"

Carl, now visibly frustrated, asked, "Are what two related?"

Cole held the advantage. "Last night and the guy getting his head knocked."

"Not that I can tell. Where were you two nights ago, Cole?"

Tony cut in, "You seem more concerned about one guy."

Carl stared at both of them, taking a moment to calm himself. He pushed his jacket aside to expose his badge and a pistol on his belt. "I investigate every crime, and I'll do it in whatever goddamned order I want."

Tony had a calmness about him that Cole knew hid a furious yet strategic pace of his own questions. Tony took a sip, put his cup down and crossed his legs. "How many died last night?"

Carl replied in a matter-of-fact tone. "Sixteen that we know of." He then turned to Cole and asked, "Were you downtown by chance, Cole?"

"Yeah. I saw it."

Carl pressed, "Were you downtown two nights ago?"

"Yup."

"Green Sleeves?"

"Yup."

"You see anything that you might want to tell me about?"

"Nope."

In the silence that followed, Carl cleaned his teeth with his tongue, exhaling through his nose and doing a poor job of hiding his sour mood.

Tony pressed, "So, about these drugs…"

Carl cut him off abruptly. "What about drugs? Look around, Tony. Kids do drugs. Fishermen do drugs. Hell, half of Newfoundland does drugs."

Calmly, Tony asked, "But sixteen dead bodies?"

Carl replied, "I'll get to the bottom of it. Why are you so concerned about drugs?"

Tony paused, swallowed, and replied, "Sixteen bodies, Carl, that's why."

Not getting the answers he hoped for, Carl snarled, "Well, I should be going then."

———

With the house empty again, Tony and Cole sat for some time.

Tony broke the silence, "Is that what happened to your arm?"

"He started it."

"For fuck's sake, Cole."

"What, he did. I wasn't looking for a fight."

Tony looked at him, then back out the window. "Well, you found one, didn't you?"

"Can I go now?"

Tony laughed. "No; someone's coming in the next hour to talk with you."

Cole's frustration nearly got the best of him. He shuddered and wanted to get out of that house and clear his mind. He asked plainly, "Who?"

"A friend of mine from the governor's office, to try and get you a security clearance."

Cole thought back to his last one from the Coast Guard. It was a fairly straightforward process. He moped around the house for the next hour or until Tony answered a knock at the door. A woman, a few years older than Cole, stepped in and gave Tony a partial hug. From the couch, Cole could see immediately that she was pretty, athletic, and had seemingly sunburned blonde hair. His mood changed.

Tony invited her in. "Stacey, thanks for coming."

"No problem." As she walked, she set her purse down and Cole sensed something, an awkwardness almost, between the two. She glanced at Cole, then set her briefcase down beside a chair and took a seat. Cole leaned back in his chair, looking for a moment at the midday sun that snuck through the low clouds casting shadows down on the harbor.

"Cole, is it?"

He nodded. "Yeah; nice to meet you."

She was in work mode, having professionally cast aside whatever first impressions she'd already made of him.

"The governor has asked if we can grant you an interim clearance, so I'm going to go over a bit of your history with you and then we'll run some background checks. Shouldn't take more than a week or so."

Cole nodded. "OK."

Stacey pulled out a notepad. "So let's get to this. Can you tell me your job history, starting from ten years back?"

Cole looked at Tony for some reassurance, and he nodded for Cole to go ahead.

"OK, well, I was in the Coast Guard."

She asked, "For how long?"

"Six years. I was at the Coast Guard Academy in Connecticut, then two years on a ship out of New Hampshire."

Stacey took notes and asked for addresses, with Cole surprised that he could still remember. She jotted them down, looked at him for a moment, then leaned her head slightly forward, "And then?"

Cole thought for a moment on how best to sum up his life from there.

"I got fired."

She stopped writing and looked up. "How did that go?"

Cole was embarrassed. He looked at Tony, who smiled, and said softly, "Better tell her."

Cole took a breath, rubbed at his cheek, and dove in.

"My command and I didn't exactly see eye to eye, so they arranged to have me separated from the Coast Guard."

She thought for a moment about what to write in her notes. "What happened then?"

"I worked on a tour boat out of Key West for a while."

"How long were you in Key West?"

"Until I went to Panama."

"Why did you go to Panama?"

Cole thought for a moment, unsure of where to even start. He'd already glossed over so much. *Fuck it*, he thought.

Under his breath, he spoke, "Well, here we go…"

"Here what goes?"

Cole laughed to himself and looked at Stacey, holding back the devilish grin that wanted desperately to sneak out from his otherwise expressionless face. "I went to Panama to run drugs."

She looked up from her notes, then to Tony, then back at Cole. "Why?"

"Because I was tired of smuggling migrants."

He relished in her discomfort, knowing that he'd only skimmed the surface of his story. She wrote long and detailed notes for some time before asking him to continue.

Cole then detailed Martinique, then Key West again, then Panama City, and finally France. She wrote again for some time.

"How did you get from Martinique to Key West?"

"I got arrested."

She chewed at her lower lip and took a long deep breath. "Who arrested you?"

Tony smiled when Cole looked at him. "He did."

Stacey asked, "Who did?"

"Tony."

She turned to Tony, "You arrested him?"

Tony nodded.

"For what?"

Cole chimed in, "I had a lot of cocaine with me, until I burned it."

She asked, "Is that the only time you've been arrested?"

"Not exactly."

"There are others?"

Cole looked at Tony, and asked, "Carentan?"

Tony rolled his head from side to side, then replied, "You weren't technically arrested that time."

Cole thought, then nodded with some certainty. "Yeah. I think that's the only time I've actually been arrested."

"Any other trouble with law enforcement?"

"Well…" He didn't know where to go with that one.

She waited patiently, tapping her pen against her yellow legal notepad.

Looking at Tony, Cole said, "Mexico?"

Tony cut in. "We can't really discuss Mexico here."

Confused and looking at both of them, she asked, "You didn't mention Mexico."

"Sorry; I forgot about that."

Tony cut in again. "Please don't write that down, Stacey."

She put her pen down and looked at Tony for several seconds, then turned to Cole. "Where and when have you committed any criminal acts, regardless of whether you were caught or not?"

Cole looked at Tony, who interjected, "No details, just places?"

She was clearly frustrated. "Sure, we can start there."

"Go for it, Cole."

He thought for a few seconds, then listed them all. Key West, Cuba, Panama, Martinique, Cozumel, and finally Virginia.

At that, Tony asked, "Virginia?"

He replied, "Speeding," then shrugged his shoulders.

Tony blinked a few times, then asked, "Was that the thing with Claire?"

Cole turned to the woman and smiled. "I didn't get caught that time, but they may be looking for me."

She wrote as Tony and Cole sat awkwardly in silence. After that, she re-read her three pages of notes and thought some more. "Who did you smuggle drugs for in Panama?"

Cole was in his element now. "He's dead."

"Who is dead?"

"The guy I was working for."

"How did he die?"

"I killed him."

Tony cut in again. "OK, please don't write that down either." He thought for a moment, then continued. "I think Mexico and Panama may need to stay off the record."

She looked up at Cole. "Did you kill someone in Mexico, too?"

Cole said nothing, knowing that only he knew the truth behind what had gone down in Mexico. He thought about Johnson briefly and the sound of gravel flinging itself up and out from the undercarriage of the Thing.

Tony patted his thighs and ran his hands up and his pant leg a few times. "This may have been a bad idea."

She defended the whole thing, saying, "The governor asked me to come out here today, but I don't see us, or the U.S. for that matter, giving you an interim clearance, let alone a permanent one."

Looking at Tony with some level of frustration and hopelessness on her face, she asked, "Can we speak upstairs?"

They left Cole alone for a few minutes. Some time passed before she made her way back downstairs and to the front door. Tony came down behind her.

"Thanks for coming over. Sorry we couldn't work that out."

From the couch, Cole caught her eyes as they looked at him with some level of curiosity. He smiled and asked, "Wanna get a drink sometime?"

She looked away from him, the curiosity immediately gone from her face, and opened the front door to walk out. Tony closed it behind her, and he was scowling now too.

"Did you have to ask her out?"

Cole shrugged. "What?"

"She's from the governor's office. I'm trying not to burn any bridges there."

Cole pressed, "She's cute, right?"

Tony laughed. "Yeah, she's a cutie."

They both sat at the couch and stared out the window. It was mid-afternoon now, and a light breeze had picked up down on the channel outside.

Cole asked, "So no clearance, huh?"

Tony shook his head. "Not a chance."

"Does that mean I have to leave?"

"Nah. Maybe it's best if you stay off the books on this one anyhow."

"Was I ever on the books to begin with?"

Tony looked at him and smiled. "No. And that's never stopped you, now, has it?"

CHAPTER 7: THE UNFORTUNATE ONES

COLE WALKED DOWNTOWN with the fading afternoon light. By the time he rounded the corner up past YellowBelly towards George Street, the evening chill had once again blanketed Newfoundland. He ducked inside Green Sleeves and waved at the bartender, exchanging a somber nod with him. Seated by the corner of the bar, Cole soon held a stout in his hand and the bartender hung back to see if Cole was in the mood to chat.

"Damn shame," Cole said as he took his first sip.

The bartender, about Cole's age, tossed a hand towel under the bar and crossed his arms as he leaned against the back of the bar.

"Sure is."

Cole asked, "Did you know any of them?"

Under his thick dark beard, Cole caught a grimace spreading across his lips as he replied, "I did, a few of them. Not close, but one of the kids was a neighbor of mine. We were in school together."

Cole nodded his head in understanding. There wasn't much to say, and the bartender walked off before the silence turned awkward. Around the bar, there was a normal early-evening crowd. The people of Newfoundland were still processing, or mourning, or trying in vain to wrap their minds around what had transpired. Cole understood grief and its many complicated stages. Looking around, the almost-normal feeling in the bar told him the worst was still to come for many of them.

He gestured for another beer and when the bartender brought it to him, Cole leaned in, asking, "Where do you buy drugs around here?"

The question caught the young guy completely off guard. "You can't be serious."

"Not to buy any, but I want to know where."

The bartender paused, in defense of his island. He stared at Cole to dig a little deeper and see just where Cole was going with it.

He scanned up and back along the length of the bar before leaning closer into Cole. "You can get it anywhere on George Street. It's our blessing and our curse."

Cole nodded. "But where does it come in? I'm not talking about the street dealers."

"How would I know that?"

"Because you're a bartender. At Green Sleeves. I know you know."

The bartender looked away and buried the sly smile that almost escaped.

Cole pressed further, "Just point me in the right direction."

"Fishing boats." He paused. "That's just my guess."

Cole asked, "Airplanes?"

"Wouldn't know anything about that."

"But you do know about fishing boats?"

"It's Cole, right?"

Cole nodded.

"I've had buddies that worked on the boats from time to time. I've heard some stories. That's all."

"Fair enough." He changed the subject. "Music still on tonight?"

"Should be."

Cole smiled and finished his beer. His mind was racing with a plan, and he felt some relief in making what little progress he could.

"I'll swing by later. Thanks."

He walked a wandering course down to the wharf, along its long lonely length and made note of the darkest alleys and hiding places. There were too many shadows to keep track of them all, but he was laying out a map in his mind, like Matt and Harley had shown him in Cozumel, figuring that he may need it later. It was just after nine in the evening, and he thought about heading for Tony's, and just as quickly he thought about Olivia. He worked his way back up the hill towards YellowBelly.

Once inside, he was down the winding stairs to the UnderBelly a minute later. She was at the bar and smiled when he sat down. She sent a compassionate look his way, and he felt as if he'd just learned a great deal about the girl. Even at rest, the darkness of her lips, her hair, and her curves under what was no doubt a carefully selected outfit offered a savage and erotic portrait of a young woman, but Cole was increasingly certain that underneath her armor she carried a warm heart.

"Beer?"

He smiled. "Yeah, please. How're you holding up?"

From across the bar, she shrugged her shoulders as if she didn't know what to say. Once back closer to him, she leaned against the bar and waited for him to ask his question again.

He looked right into her eyes. "How are you?"

She thought for a moment. "I'm all right."

"Your friends?"

She said nothing, and Cole knew immediately that like so many others living in small towns, the deaths had hit home. He reached out and held her hand, squeezing it a few times to shake her from whatever thought or memory had crawled into her head.

She looked at him, her fingers now squeezing his hand in return. "My cousin. I used to babysit her."

Cole bit at his upper lip, exhaled, and replied, "I'm sorry."

Olivia didn't acknowledge him. Instead, she continued on with the thought. "I knew she had a fake ID."

Cole knew immediately that she blamed herself. It was a more advanced stage of grief, and one that he'd wrestled with many times on his own. His mind raced with ways to pull her back out.

"I'm getting involved."

She looked up at him and tilted her head. "How?"

"I've done some work in the past rooting this kind of stuff out. What do you know about where these pills come from?"

She shook her head. "I don't know. It's a different generation. When I was a teen, we smoked pot and drank our parents' whiskey. I don't know much about pills."

Cole pressed her. "Boats?"

She shrugged. It was true; she really didn't know. He squeezed at her hand again, now just for the sake of his own comfort more than hers. They both smiled at the underlying hints that seemed to inadvertently float in each other's direction.

He asked, "You ever heard of a kid named Timmy?"

She shook her head, but she was still thinking about it.

Cole continued, "Little kid, small frame, dances around like a freak at the clubs at night?"

"The gay kid?"

Cole smiled. "That's the one."

She asked, "How do you know him?"

"I've seen him around." He turned the question on her, "How do *you* know him?"

She took a breath. "My cousin hung out with him from time to time. I've seen them around downtown. I just always assumed he was harmless." She paused. "What did he do?"

Cole licked at his lips. "I think he may have had those pills on him that night."

"You know how to find him?"

"No."

"Where did your cousin hang out?"

"All the kids sneak into Allure. Other than that, they wandered a lot, the back alleys and places where seventeen-year-olds go when they can't get in a club."

Her eyes were wandering back and forth in thought before her words caught up with her. "There's a warehouse off Duckworth where

I think they have a way in. We used to do the same thing when I was in school."

Cole let go of her hand and took a long sip from his beer, looking around the bar. It was quiet for this late at night. Olivia was now staring off at the far wall, her chin sunk into her hand with an elbow resting on the bar. He felt guilty for thinking about how pretty she was. Her head was no more than a foot from his, the two of them more or less alone in the dim light. He leaned over to her, his outstretched palm against the side of her neck and his fingers resting behind her ear. He pulled gently and kissed her on the side of her cheek, holding them in an embrace.

When he let go, she didn't move much, but her eyes locked directly on his. If she was surprised, she didn't show it.

He rested his hand on top of hers. "It hurts for a while. Don't run away from that."

She asked, "What do you mean?"

"It's normal to feel what you're feeling. You gotta let it run its course."

She motioned quietly with her mouth. "Thanks."

He turned his focus back to the warehouse, asking, "How do I find that warehouse?"

"Two blue doors on the alley. There's no knobs on them, but one of them you can pry open from the outside."

"Good."

"Cole," she said with some hesitation in her voice.

"What?"

"Be careful."

"I will." He stood up, finishing his beer and setting the glass back down.

He asked, "How about lunch one day?"

She smiled for a moment. "I'd like that."

It didn't take Cole long to find the two blue doors. He'd wandered the darkest of the alleyways for half an hour before stumbling across the one he was looking for. Standing for a few moments, he took deep breaths to slow his heartrate. Finding a crowbar in the rubble by the first door, he reckoned this was the one to pry open. In his bare hands, it was cold and heavy, giving him reason to pause one last time and question what he was about to do.

He thought first of Olivia, then back to the dying girl in the snow. He slid the blade of the crowbar in, trying not to make too much noise. It creaked as he pulled against it. Bits of rust fell to the ground as the heavy door began to angle open. A moment later, he slid his fingers in and opened it the rest of the way. As he did, the hinges groaned and Cole grit his teeth, fearing that he'd alerted anyone inside to his presence. Inside, the bare hallway was dark with a turn to the left at the end. He stood for another minute then told himself if teenagers could do it, so could he.

He gently let the door close behind him and was blinded by the darkness until his eyes adjusted and the faintest glow appeared from around the corner. The hall smelled of stagnant water and trash. He walked to the end and stopped just short of the turn. Peering around the corner, he could see two exposed light bulbs hanging near the far wall. Neither cast enough light to see the entirety of the cavernous space inside. In a far corner, he heard water dripping, but little else disturbed the stagnant damp air.

Walking carefully into the large space, he sidestepped to his right to clear himself from the doorway. He felt alone, vulnerable even, amid the ghostly shadows. As his eyes adjusted, he was able to take in more features from the space. There were some old ragged seats around a loose circle by one wall and piles of trash. Cole took a breath and smelled the hint of a smoldering fire.

He walked closer to the chairs along the far wall, and stopped ten feet short of them. His eyes were fixed on a thin and sickly looking hand draped over the armrest, its palm upwards and fingertips curled. Cole's lungs had seized, and he was unable to inhale. Chills started in his jaw then ran to the back of his neck and down the length of his back.

"Hello?"

There was no reply. Even under the dim light, he could see two thick blue veins on the surface of the lifeless wrist.

"Hello?"

There was still no reply. *Dammit,* Cole thought. He walked another five feet, taking a circular route to keep some distance from the body slumped clumsily in the chair. As he got closer, he blinked twice and fought hard to swallow the lump in the back of his throat. He took in the sight in front of him. They were all dead, of that much he was certain.

Several were on the floor, curled up on filthy damp rugs. If there had ever been patterns on the rugs, they had long ago been masked by the grease and dirt, the water and the mud. Four more of the chairs were filled with lifeless bodies, their heads tilted to the side or back, their mouths open from their last gasps for air. The crusted foam on some of their lips told Cole they hadn't been dead for long. He walked delicately among the detritus and counted roughly eight, all bone-thin with ragged faces and sunken eyes. They were no doubt the hardened addicts of St. John's, the unfortunate ones most often unseen or otherwise ignored by the nighttime masses. Cole had seen them from time to time, begging for spare change on George Street or arguing with street lamps until being chased away by a bouncer. They were the ones who'd fallen victim to the unending debauchery of a party town. Two of them, a man and woman, were wrapped in what amounted to a hug on one of the rugs.

On the far side of the bodies, a smoldering pile of trash revealed itself as the source of the faint smoke. He walked over and crouched down, holding his hand just inches above the grey and black ashes. There was a hint of warmth left from whomever had last stoked the fire. From his crouched position, Cole turned to the back of the room, near the door where he had walked in, and he heard the pattering of heavy footsteps hitting puddles on the floor. He stood and pivoted quickly, stayed low, and watched as a figure dashed across the dark space. As he rounded a corner, the figure slid and fell, letting out a youthful grunt.

Timmy, Cole thought. Cole was up and sprinting towards the door. The kid wouldn't get away so easily this time. Cole was out the door moments after Timmy and he sprinted full speed down a narrow alley. Cole was gaining on him, his lungs on fire, and he was once again amazed at how quick the kid moved. A hundred yards further, Timmy fell again for no apparent reason. He was up a second later and regaining his pace before he collapsed once more.

Cole caught up as Timmy was trying to stand up, but seemed stuck in a contorted prone position. He made puking noises a moment later and Cole rolled him to his side. Twice more Timmy's chest contorted until he finally threw up a mess of bile and pills onto the pavement. There were no less than two dozen pills now spread out on the alleyway.

Cole asked, "Where'd they come from?"

Timmy shook his head, clutching at his stomach as he threw up another dozen pills.

"For fuck's sake, Timmy. Why did you do this?"

"They're all dead," he said, disbelief and fear spread across his thin pale face. The whites of his eyes were red as they rolled back and he made more puking sounds.

"Timmy, where did they come from?"

He softly mouthed the word, "Who?"

"The drugs, Timmy. Where did you get them?"

Timmy looked away and buried his face into the cold concrete. He was sweating now, steam once again rising off his soaked and soiled black cotton shirt. As Cole held him down with one arm, Timmy began violently shaking.

"Timmy, I need to know where you got the drugs."

He couldn't be sure if it was a seizure or hypothermia, but Timmy was getting worse by the second.

"Timmy, the drugs—where did you get them?"

Timmy clenched his jaw and tried to roll, fighting with the little bit of strength left to wrestle free from Cole. He let his grip go as Timmy settled once more onto his side and clutched both his arms against his chest. Veins bulged out from his gaunt neck as he slipped into another round of convulsions.

"Timmy."

Timmy lifted his head slightly off the ground, and mouthed something before letting his head back down and taking a gasp for air.

"Timmy."

He looked at Cole with a deathly expression and opened his mouth, paused, then grit his teeth and spoke, "*North Star.*"

Cole asked, "What is that?"

Timmy said it again, "*North Star.*"

"Is that where the pills came from?"

Timmy took a long breath, and mouthed, "I didn't know they were bad…"

He shook violently once more and his chest surged as his stomach turned again.

Cole rested his hand on Timmy's shoulder, "I'll go get help; hang on."

Timmy didn't respond.

Cole patted him once more and hopped up, running back up the alley to the main road. He ran hard to find a pub or restaurant that was open, but he knew by the time the paramedics got there, Timmy would likely be dead.

CHAPTER 8: OUTLAW

A WHITE SHEET WAS spread over Timmy, hues of red and blue reflecting off the wet pavement from the ambulance and police cars up at the entrance of the alley. Cole had called from a pub then ran for Tony's. Now the two of them stood to the side as police stood idly by outside the blue door at the further end of the alley. Cole had his hands buried deep in the pockets of his jacket and lifted his head upwards as the steam blew out from between his lips.

Tony asked, "Was he trying to kill himself?"

Cole, his head still up as the last bits of steam slipped upwards from his mouth and spun in circles until disappearing into the night, thought for a moment before replying. "Yeah; pretty sure."

"Drug dealer with a conscience, huh?"

Cole nodded. "He was just a kid who killed his friends with bad pills."

As they stood there in the alley, the blue door swung open and half a dozen police officers emerged, most of them headed for the other officers milling about. One walked towards Cole, and when he got there, he nodded at Tony and sniffled before wiping at his nose.

"There were another six in a backroom."

Cole asked, "Dead?"

"Yup."

Tony chimed in, "What's the total?"

"We found fifteen. Looks like the bulk of the hardcore addicts went down with this one."

"You know them?"

The officer almost smiled at Cole. "Yeah. When someone is as far along as they are, or were, we end up seeing them quite a bit."

The three of them stood for a few moments before the officer started in on Cole with the questions.

"What were you doing in there?"

"I heard Timmy may be in there."

"Why did you want to meet Timmy?"

"I figured he had something to do with the pills."

"Why didn't you come to us first?"

Cole looked at Tony for some help, but Tony just shrugged. As he did, the three of them turned at the sound of Carl's hoarse voice coming down the alley. The officer turned and greeted him, saying, "Detective, I was just asking him some questions about..."

Carl cut him off. "That will be all."

The ensuing awkward silence lasted a few seconds before the officer turned and walked back to the other cops.

Carl's gaze never left Cole. "What the fuck are you doing here?"

Cole, his dislike for Carl now cemented in his mind, replied, "I was looking for Timmy."

"Why?"

"I met him the other night."

"So you were trying to meet a fag in an abandoned warehouse?"

It didn't phase Cole. He looked back at the sheet once more, nodded and replied, "I wanted to talk with him."

Carl demanded, "Why?"

Cole lied. "He had a cute friend."

"Boy or a girl?"

For the first time since meeting him, Cole had the fleeting thought that he just might have to kill Carl at some point. He steadied his nerves and replied, "A girl."

Carl thought for a few moments, his ruddy cheeks still the most prominent feature of his otherwise disgruntled face. Even under the faintest light from the streetlight above them, Carl was undoubtedly pissed off.

He turned to Tony, asking, "What are you doing here?"

Tony tried to calm things down as best as he could, answering, "Cole came and got me."

Turning back to Cole, Carl changed his tone. "I could arrest you."

Cole said nothing.

"In fact, I might arrest you. I haven't decided yet. Neither of you go anywhere." Carl marched down to the assembled police.

Tony stood silent for a minute, thinking of the right words.

"Stay clear of him, Cole."

Cole nodded. "I'm trying."

Tony asked, "Did the kid say anything?"

Cole debated letting Tony in. A year ago, Cole wouldn't have told anyone a thing. But he trusted Tony and took a calming breath before answering.

"*North Star.*"

"Huh?"

"He said *North Star*, does that mean anything to you?"

Tony ran his tongue across the front of his upper teeth and nodded, staring back up the street. "It's a boat."

"One you're watching?"

"Yup. It's up there on the priority list."

"Drugs?"

Tony rubbed at his nose and looked for a long second at Cole. "Among other things, yeah."

"So I need that clearance for you to tell me more?"

Tony laughed. "You don't have a fart's chance in a hurricane of getting a clearance." He paused and patted Cole on the back. "We'll talk more back at the house."

———

Carl had thankfully cut them loose, and the two of them sat in the living room as the early morning hours approached. Cole had worked up two cups of Irish coffee, bastardized by the heavy preponderance of whiskey. Tony smiled and laughed after taking his first sip.

"I wasn't ready for that."

Cole feigned ignorance. "Huh?"

"The whiskey."

"Sorry."

"Nah, it's good. I kind of needed it."

Shaking the chill from his shoulders, Cole took a good long sip and leaned back into the couch. Neither of them were ready to talk, so Cole stared intently outside at the darkness as another bitter night passed. Two more long sips and the warmth had returned to his fingers. He pressed the pads of his thumbs against each individual finger to stop the stinging.

"The governor is under the impression I'm here to follow drugs moving back and forth across the Atlantic. We have his full support for that mission."

"But?"

Tony laughed and drank down half the mug, holding the coffee and whiskey in his mouth for a few moments before he swallowed. It was his turn to stare out the window. Cole didn't disturb him. He could tell Tony was deep in thought by the rapid movement of his eyes. When they finally settled down, he was fixated on the far cliffs of the channel. Only the white fingers of snow draped over the black rock was visible through the darkness.

"What do you know about Irish politics?"

Cole thought for a moment. "Not much."

"Well, it's getting a little heated over there."

"How?"

"Ever hear about the IRA?"

Cole nodded. "Yeah. I thought that was, like, decades ago."

"There's a small group that's trying to bring it back, a New-Irish Republican Army."

"What does that have to do with St. John's?"

Tony paused again, Cole knowing that Tony was wrestling with how much he could tell him. In all likelihood, he'd said too much already. "They're trying to smuggle in weapons."

Cole still wasn't putting the pieces together. His expression told Tony as much and he continued. "There's been some movement of guns, pistols and rifles mostly along with ammunition, out of New England via the commercial fishing fleet. The Coast Guard busted one of them a month ago." He paused to see if Cole was following. "It had charts for Newfoundland."

Cole had enough pieces of the puzzle now. Newfoundland was a staging area, a stopover before making the jump across the Atlantic.

Tony continued, "It's still a bit fuzzy, but the drugs are part of it, I just don't know how they tie into it all. There's been an uptick in drugs, too, and most of them are pretty low quality."

It made sense, given the more than two dozen dead in the past week.

Cole asked, "Anyone else know?"

"Here?"

"Anywhere."

Tony stared at him, and answered, "Back home, there's a small team working this as a side project. It's still pretty compartmentalized and unfunded. The only U.S. interest is the guns; they're coming from America. If the past months are any indication, we're about due for another shipment…"

Cole asked, "What's our job?"

Tony tilted his head, mulling over his answer.

"We're just here to monitor right now."

Tony looked intently at him, as if to acknowledge that he knew all too well that Cole wasn't one to sit back and watch.

He slept until midday, waking up in a fairly good mood. He made it out
to the kitchen and rustled up some breakfast before his mind wandered
and he found himself stuck on thoughts of Isabella and Marie.

"Dammit," he said softly under his breath.

Outside, the air was still under a heavy blanket of low-hanging grey
clouds. As soon as he finished breakfast, Cole was out the door and ran
up to Signal Hill and back. Outside Tony's house an hour later, his
lungs burned as he took heavy breaths. Beads of sweat stung his eyes,
but otherwise the salt had dried up on the rest of his face and exposed
hands in the winter air.

An hour later, he was out the door and down to George Street.
Olivia wouldn't be at work for some time, but he knew that sitting
around Tony's would only dredge up more thoughts about Isabella.
That scared him, so he opted to walk along the waterfront and think of
other things. Half the fleet was out given the relatively good weather
over the past two days, and the wharf was quiet. A third of the way up
towards the east end of the harbor, he stopped when he came across a
blue hull, its name in small gold letters on the stern, *North Star*.

Cole stood for a few seconds, looking her over. As he did, a young
man emerged from the inside and stepped out onto the rotting wooden
deck.

"Howdy."

The man stared at Cole, unsure of how to reply. "Hey," was all he
said.

"What are you looking for?"

Cole snapped himself out of the trance he was in and replied,
"Sorry, just out for a walk, I was just looking at boats. Sorry to bother
you."

He retreated quickly to a bar overlooking the wharf. Ordering a
Guinness, Cole took a seat that afforded him a full view of the *North
Star*. The crewmember didn't appear again for another hour. When he
did, he was on a phone for a few minutes before ducking back inside.
Cole was on his third beer when another scruffy man appeared,

climbed over the rail, and onto the deck of the boat. The first guy with whom Cole had spoken stepped out and the two of them talked for a minute before he walked off and headed back up the wharf.

Fearing that he was drawing too much attention to himself, Cole ordered a burger and spent the next hour waiting patiently and pretending to enjoy his fries one by one. As darkness finally settled, he gave up and paid his tab. Back up on George Street, the mood felt different. At Green Sleeves, there was quiet music on in the background and only a handful of patrons seated at the corner tables.

The bartender made her way over to Cole as he sat down. For a moment, he felt as if she was upset with him even being there.

"Water?"

She nodded, turned and walked back over to the far side of the bar, returning a minute later and pushing a tall glass in front of him.

"Thanks."

She walked back to the far side and leaned against a beam, seemingly trying her best to blend in against the wall, her arms crossed in front of her. Cole didn't dare try to make conversation with her. He suspected she, like most of St. John's, had some connection to someone who'd overdosed.

The stage was bare and he wondered if they'd booked music for the evening. The bartender wasn't making much effort to move, so Cole finished his glass, tapped it on the table, and when she looked at him, he smiled and threw her a half-assed salute as he stood and walked for the door. From there, he made his way to Olivia at the UnderBelly.

As he sat, she asked, "How are you?"

"I could ask you the same thing."

"I'm all right," she said with a mostly genuine smile.

"Beer?"

"Stout, if you've got it."

She laughed, turned, and poured him a pint. Setting it down in front of him, she leaned in and waited to see what he had to say. Unsure of where to start, he reached out and patted her hand with his to buy

himself some time. She looked at him with that same vicious and seductive expression, her eyes piercing his as if they could effortlessly
bore deep into the thoughts spinning around in his mind.

He hoped that she couldn't in fact read his mind, lest she know the
immediate and overwhelming lust that consumed his brain. She tilted
her head, and as she did, thick strands of her dark hair slipped over her
shoulder and partially concealed the side of her face. He leaned further
in and was even more confident when she didn't seem to object. He was
close enough to smell her perfume and took a slow deep breath, finding
comfort in something familiar.

Half playfully, she asked, "What are you doing, Cole?"

"Flirting. Is that all right?"

She smiled. "Yeah, but I wish you'd flirt a little bit faster."

He couldn't help but smile back at her.

"But what I mean is what are you doing here, in St. John's?"

It was a legitimate question and one that carried a complicated answer.

"I'm gonna work on this pill thing."

She pulled her head back slightly, her eyes narrowing, and looked
at him, biting at her lower lip.

"How?" She paused and followed up with a confused, "Why?"

"I dunno. It's something I'm good at. I've got some experience with
these kinds of things."

"But why?"

The question had a complex answer and one that Cole wasn't entirely comfortable sharing with her. Perhaps it was the fear of monot-
ony, perhaps it was a sense of purpose, but for whatever reason Cole
was intrigued by the whole thing, the uncertainty of it, the danger, the
cold North Atlantic that seemed to call him from just beyond the cliffs
of the harbor. He didn't have all the pieces put together yet, but it would
give him something to pour his energy into. Either way, he preferred
action to idleness. And perhaps he could beat back his daily demons
with something constructive, or destructive if need be. And perhaps, at

the very root of his mischievous soul, he knew that he stood a good chance of stirring up some trouble for a worthy cause.

He rested his hand on hers again and leaned in, looking to his left and across the bar at the half-dozen patrons that were minding their own business. He tilted his head to the right, motioning for her to come in closer. When she did, they were no more than a few inches from each other. He wasted no time, leaning in and kissing her delicate lips. She turned her head towards him and away from the rest of the bar. The darkness of the walls gave them the benefit of some intimacy for the moment. Her lips were soft, and he touched his tongue gently against hers for a brief second before pulling back.

She gave no hint as to whether she approved or disapproved, her eyes locked on his, and he relished the near-instant explosion in his heart. The left outermost corner of her lip curled upwards for a brief second before she reclaimed her stoic pose, her dark eyes never leaving his. A lesser man would have crumbled right there at her feet.

"Can you get me a gun?"

She held her gaze, asking coldly, "Is that why you just kissed me?"

He shook his head. "No. That just kind of happened."

She lowered her chin and tilted her head. "Unplanned. How romantic you are."

"I was going to kiss you at some point. Should I apologize?"

"Would you?"

He grinned. "Probably not."

She stared at him as the beating of his heart was picking up again. She played a wicked game, and Cole wondered if she even knew how good she was at it. After what seemed like an eternity, she smiled, unlocking him from her eyes.

"This is Canada. We don't have guns like you do in America."

"I know, but you do have guns."

She leaned closer to him. "I don't have any guns, Cole."

"But can you find one?"

"Why?"

He thought for a moment. "I might need it."

Finishing his beer, he set it down and looked at her once more. The last ten minutes had been something special, and he didn't want to overstay his welcome. Moreover, he wanted to check the wharf one more time.

"I should go. Can we meet up tomorrow?"

She sighed. "Tomorrow is not good. There are services for some of the people that died."

"Gotcha."

"How about in two days?"

Cole nodded. "Yeah. Whenever you're around."

"All right; let's get lunch. I'll meet you at noon at Duke of Duckworth. You know where that is?"

"I do." He paused then stood up, resting his hand once more on top of hers and gently squeezed her hand.

"See ya."

CHAPTER 9: THE BROKER

IT WAS MID-MORNING as Cole sat on the couch with Tony across from him in a chair. He was interested in what Cole was saying, and he took that as a good sign. He'd been back down to the wharf and hung out among the shadows of a crumbling brick wall, his hands deep in his pockets as he stared across a gravel lot at the *North Star*. Freezing cold, he'd been close to giving up and walking home when he first saw the car. Its lights out, the sedan had pulled right up to the boat. Cole watched as two men unloaded cases from the open trunk and manhandled them up and over the gunwale to the waiting crewmember. There were less than a dozen cases, most similar in size to the Pelican cases Harley and Matt had lugged to Cozumel. In situations like this, Cole knew Pelican cases carried one thing—weapons.

Tony asked, "What size?"

Cole replied, "Rifles."

"Twelve ain't enough to make a trip across the Atlantic."

Cole smirked. "I'll watch again tonight."

Tony stared at him for a moment before adding, "We'll watch them tonight."

"You don't trust me?"

"I trust you, Cole…"

Cole didn't know what to say and stumbled to find the right words. He knew Tony only meant to help and reassured him, "It's all good. I could use the help."

The two of them sat there, Tony staring out the window with one leg draped over the other. He was deep in thought, and Cole didn't dare disturb him, knowing that Tony would formulate a far more precise plan than anything he could. Tony's plans were always strategic, whereas Cole knew he worked best at the tactical level, his mind wandering haphazardly from one fucked up situation to the next. Cole also knew that he his niche seemed to be doing the things that others couldn't stomach.

The *North Star* was getting prepped to run weapons, of that both Cole and Tony were certain. If she was tied into the drugs as well, a complicated web of the international underworld would need to be mapped out. Cole didn't have the drive to accomplish such a task, but he knew Tony did.

"We'll head downtown at dusk, get some food, and wait."

Cole grinned. "Sounds good to me. Anything until then?"

"Can you stay out of trouble?"

"Probably."

"I mean it, Cole. You need to lay low."

"I'll take a walk."

Tony seemed relieved, and Cole walked to his room, dressed for an afternoon hike up the hill and back before unceremoniously leaving out the front door. Once outside, he felt good. He shivered and picked up his pace as he made his way east down the Battery, squinting at the sunlight ricocheting off the frozen icy piles of plowed snow. He stepped off the wooden deck and onto the trail, hopping from stone to stone almost at a jog until he felt the first drip of sweat on the center of his chest. From there, he worked back to a manageable pace to keep his core warm but below the threshold of breaking into a full sweat. He was at the top of Signal Hill before he knew it and caught his breath. It was still mid-afternoon and too early to head back. Without some activity, Cole knew he would sit, and his idle mind would take him places he preferred not to go.

To the north, the trails continued in less discernible paths. The sun was hours from setting, so he pushed onward, past the small crowds at the tower and soon he was alone among the undisturbed white snow and grey rock. A stiff wind blew in from the east against the cliffs and carried with it bits of spray and foam from the Atlantic below. Despite the wind, which stung at his exposed face, Cole was warm and he found a clarity in the solitude that had escaped him for months. The trail wandered gently up and down the rolling terrain, hugging near-vertical drops of nearly 1,000 feet. The combination of risks and rewards left him feeling more alive than he had in quite some time. Letting his mind wander, he thought back to Cozumel and didn't fight against his conscience as it dwelled on those shadows from his past.

Nearly an hour later, he stopped on a high bluff and exhaled, his breath thrown back in his face by the incessant wind. He breathed deep with his heartbeat thumping. He felt as if he would be all right. As the thought took hold, his mind turned to Timmy's guilt. It felt odd to dwell on it, but the anguish in the kid's face as he puked up pills and died of an overdose was too powerful of an image to release. Cole committed himself to exacting some kind of revenge. It was a perfectly fucked-up goal. Timmy, the teenaged drug dealer, falling victim to some faceless broker of bad pills and Cole the one to settle the score. He grit his teeth and let a small smile spread across his face before he turned for home. *A plan*, at last.

Back at the house, Cole waited patiently as Tony paced around his room upstairs. He knew by the sounds of Tony's footsteps that something was brewing. An hour later, Tony walked downstairs, and the two of them grabbed jackets and set out for downtown. They made their way down to Shamrock City and ordered food at the bar. Tony ordered water while Cole opted for his usual Guinness.

"Cole…"

He took his first sip. "What?"

"You make me nervous sometimes."

"I won't kill anyone, OK?"

Tony stared at him, knowing there would be some caveat to Cole's statement.

Cole looked away, taking a second sip, and mumbled under his breath, "Tonight."

Tony rubbed at his eyes, shaking his head. They each ordered a plate of fish and chips and leaned back in their wooden chairs. Half an hour passed before Cole noticed Ryan in the corner, drinking his glass of straight whiskey. Neither of them were doing much more than wasting time, so Cole went over to say hello.

"How ya been?"

Ryan took another long sip, leaving nothing but ice in his glass as he held up and shook it for the bartender. He burped under his breath and rolled his head to Cole. He was clearly drunk.

Cole asked, "You all right?"

Gruffly, Ryan replied, "Yeah, I'm good."

Cole took in Ryan's state and felt bad for him.

"You heard about the warehouse?" Ryan asked.

Cole nodded. "Yeah," guessing that Ryan had no idea he'd been there.

"My good mate from school died in there, sitting in a pile of his own piss."

"I'm sorry to hear that."

Ryan continued, "We learned to play guitar together. Smoked pot when we should've been in school, drank shitty whiskey…" He paused and looked across the room.

"I'm sorry, Ryan."

Cole knew that when someone was grieving and they talked, all you could do was let them go at whatever pace suited them. He took a seat at the dark stained stool next to Ryan and leaned in at the bar, giving a look to Tony letting him know he'd be a few minutes.

"Do you know about jumping pans?"

Cole shook his head. "No."

"When the pan ice runs up against the coast, we'd see who could run out the farthest, jumping from pan to pan. I watched a kid disappear once, right between two of them."

Cole asked, "What happened?"

Ryan looked at him like he'd missed the point, "Not a goddamn thing. He was just gone."

Ryan had nothing more to say, and Cole got the point. Sitting there, his eyes lazily unfocused on the mass of glass bottles arranged around the bar.

Ryan continued. "It was stupid, such a stupid game we'd play, but he always went further out than I could."

Cole asked, "What happened to him?"

Matter-of-factly, and with slurred speech, he said, "He got into the hard drugs. I didn't. I guess that was it."

Cole was at a loss for words. Ryan looked at his watch then across the room. From the far corner, the sound guy had a blank stare on his face as he looked at Ryan.

"Fuck," he said. "I was supposed to be on stage twenty minutes ago." Ryan stood up and walked around the small crowd to the side of the stage. He stepped up, picked his guitar up by its neck, and strapped it solemnly across his chest. The sound guy looked at Ryan for a second before he walked for the mixing board. Ryan strummed a few times and looked down at his tuner. His fingers walked a few chords and then stopped. The sound guy brought up the PA, and Ryan strummed a few more times before he stepped back and stood motionless on the back of the stage, his arms crossed over his guitar and his head down. He rubbed the palm of his hand against his chin several times, strummed an open chord two more times then stood silent again.

People had now noticed and were watching him from the high-top tables around the bar. The microphone caught a faint trace of his voice. "I can't fucking do this right now."

He put his guitar back on its stand and stepped down from the stage. His head low, he walked at a quick pace to the far back corner of the bar where he grabbed his jacket, flung it over his shoulders and left the bar. The sound guy hastily put the house music back on and slowly the bar settled back to its normal routine.

An hour later, Cole set him and Tony up at the same sports bar over-looking the wharf where he worked on yet another Guinness while Tony sipped at a cup of black coffee. Soon enough they confirmed that one crewmember was onboard. He'd emerge from below decks and pace around topside for a few minutes, smoking a cigarette, before dis-appearing below again. It was the same old surveillance game from Co-zumel, and Cole spent his time trying to surmise what was going on in Tony's mind. He wondered if perhaps Tony trained with the same folks as Harley and Matt.

"You still think about Harley much?"

Tony looked bothered by the question. A moment later, his face changed as he thought deeper into why Cole may have asked the ques-tion.

"Yeah, sure. We spent a good bit of time on the road together."

Cole was probing now. "You work like him and Matt." He paused and thought for a moment. "Actually, more like Matt."

Tony laughed, seemingly at some far-flung memory that Cole had stirred up. "Harley was a wild child," he said with fondness.

Cole smiled. "He wore these board shorts one night when he and Matt were going to fuck up a house. They were standing in the kitchen of our villa, all tactical and shit, but Harley had these ridiculous board shorts on. It drove Matt nuts."

Tony laughed out loud, the kind of deep laugh that starts out sim-ple enough but builds on itself into a fervor. "I remember those board shorts. He did the same thing in Africa once."

Cole asked, "What happened that night?"

Tony looked at Cole, smiled, and replied, "Nothing that anyone other than a few guys will ever know about. But Harley did a hell of a job, board shorts and all."

Tony changed the subject like he always did and spun on his stool to look back over at the wharf. A light snow had started falling, carried at an angle to the ground by a light but steady wind. An hour passed with still nothing materializing on the wharf. Cole was now bored with his beer and sipped slowly at his third or fourth Guinness of the night. Tony had given up on convincing Cole to drink anything else.

Lost in his own thoughts and twisting his torso slowly on his stool with both his arms pressed firmly into the bar, Cole was restless. It was a pristine piece of lacquered wood, and Cole longed for the familiarity of a worn and dilapidated bar top somewhere off George Street, where 1,000 different calloused hands had worn down the once meticulously stained wood. As he thought, he noticed Tony's focus. Spinning slowly, around, he said nothing as he watched two men step out from a sedan similar to the one Cole had seen the previous night. They both watched in silence as the crewmember emerged from below, and the driver opened the trunk. The same scenario played out from the previous night. Close to a dozen Pelican cases were passed up and over the gunwale to the crewmember onboard. The passenger from the car stood off to the side with his hands deep in his thick jacket.

"Who does that look like?" Tony asked.

Cole asked, "What?"

"The jacket."

"Dunno."

Tony didn't budge. He was frozen and staring through the window, through the snow and pale yellow light, and beyond towards the boat.

"Look closer," he said.

Cole did, and his mind raced. He shook the scattered thoughts from his mind and blinked, trying to see whatever it was Tony already knew. The figure moved slowly, shifting his weight to one side and turning to look behind him. He was too far to recognize a face, but it struck Cole immediately. *Carl.*

"Is that Carl?"

Tony looked at him for a moment, letting out a grin. "Sure looks like him, doesn't it?"

"Damn." It was all Cole could think to say.

The entire transfer took less than ten minutes with Carl sitting back down in the passenger seat before being driven off down the wharf. The *North Star* was quiet again. Tony settled the tab and they both made their way back towards the house. It was almost midnight. As they walked, Cole felt the itch to stay up a bit longer.

Tony shook his head as Cole broke off to the left and started up the hill.

"Lay low, Cole."

"Yeah, yeah. I'll behave."

Cole went up past Water Street, then to the right and up the climbing curved road past YellowBelly to the heart of George Street. Green Sleeves to his right, Cole opted for something different and found his way to the black awning of Christian's. Once inside, he smiled at the dark wooden walls, beer-stained floorboards, and disorganized memorabilia that hung from nearly everywhere. He walked upstairs to the bar set aside for harder drinking and ordered a Jack and Coke. If there was trouble to be had, he knew where to start. The bar was half filled, enough people wandering about in conversation that he couldn't make out all of the faces at once. He sipped at his drink and reflected on the day.

He soon saw a man appear from behind the bar in a yellow fisherman's jacket and matching hat. It was a 'Screeching In' ceremony, where visitors were subjected to an archaic process that, if successfully completed, would award them honorary status as a Newfoundlander. It revolved around Screech, which was, in Cole's opinion, not-so-good local rum. He frankly couldn't stand the stuff. As the man made his way into the middle of the crowd, a hush ensued and soon enough he started in with a thick Newfie accent and a half dozen folks assembled around him for their initiation. They were already well-oiled from a night of drinking and didn't seem to object when the master of the ceremony produced a frozen cod and each were ordered to kiss it. Cole watched with indifference, feeling that the entire thing made light of the harsh truth of what it meant to be a Newfie.

The energy in the room peaked as they all took their prescribed shots and repeated some kind of chant at the yellow-jacketed man's command. Cole finished his drink. He turned and walked back towards the bar to order another. As he stood waiting for the bartender, he felt a tap at his shoulder.

"Cole?"

Turning, he looked and stared at the oddly familiar face for a moment. A smile grew as he shook his head in disbelief, "Jake?"

"Yeah, man. What the hell are you doing up here?"

Cole fired the question right back at him. "What are you doing up here?"

Jake just smiled. "I'm flying Hercs. We're up here with the International Ice Patrol."

Cole didn't understand. "What the hell is that?"

Jake laughed, a kind of confidence emanating from him that Cole had never seen when they'd been stationed on *Delaney* years ago. He patted Cole hard on the back, "Damn good to see you man. So what are you doing up here?"

"Hiding out, I guess."

"What are you drinking?"

"Whiskey."

Jake motioned for two more drinks and turned to face Cole, his back leaning casually against the bar.

Jake continued, "Dude, you were like the world's most wanted man for a while. What did you get into?"

"I could tell you, but I'd have to kill you."

The bartender brought over two more, and they tapped their drinks against each other firmly, with some spilling from each of their glasses onto their hands. It was comforting to see someone familiar, and Cole thought back to their last chase together, speeding along under a nighttime sky off the Colombian coast. Any fondness for that night was quickly snuffed out by the memories that followed.

"So what's the ice thing you're doing?"

Jake took a long sip with a kind of content and easy demeanor. He looked across the room before turning his attention back to Cole.

"We're up here for a few weeks to track icebergs coming out of the Arctic. It's fucking awesome. I go sightseeing on autopilot for a few hours a day and drink my face off on George Street every night."

Cole looked out across the bar and pieced together what must have been the rest of Jake's crew. They were huddled together, one or two of them trying to ensnare any of the women that revealed even the subtlest hint of interest in them. They were all also clearly drunk.

"Those your guys?"

Jake nodded. "Yup. We're flying tomorrow, so I gotta somehow corral them back to the hotel here in a bit."

He turned back to Cole. "Seriously, what did you get into after *Delaney*?"

Fuck it, Cole thought. He finished his drink with one last sip and set the glass down firmly on the bar.

"I started running migrants. Then drugs. Then it got a little too crazy and I split. I wandered over to the eastern side of the Caribbean and got caught up in it all again. That's when y'all got me."

He didn't bring up Isabella or Marie. Those details were too personal to share at a moment like this.

Jake pushed for more. "Yeah, but after that, Potts about lost his mind. He said you went right back to it…"

Cole shook his head, smiling a bit before continuing. "Sort of. I had to clean some shit up."

Jake looked at him, Cole unsure as to whether it was admiration or disbelief.

"Guys talked about you, man. I'd hear bits and pieces at the Task Force. Where have you been since then?"

"Europe a bit, Mexico…"

Jake cut him off. "Don't tell me you were in Cozumel?"

Cole played dumb. "What happened in Cozumel?"

"A shit storm, from what I heard."

Cole laughed. "Nah, that wasn't me." Cole knew there were some things that needed to stay under the radar, even if they made for a hell of a story. "How'd you hear all that?"

Jake raised two fingers to the bartender before replying. "I was at JIATF-South for a year after *Delaney* before I got into Flight School."

He looked at Cole with what was most definitely some level of admiration. "Seriously, you're a fucking story and a half down there."

"That was a long time ago."

Jake passed him a new drink. "And now?"

"I'm just visiting for a while, laying low."

They finished their drinks and retold a few stories from their time at sea. It was well after two in the morning when Jake reluctantly sighed and said he needed to get the boys back to their hotel. They both agreed to meet up again downtown. As Jake meandered into the crowd, Cole pressed his side into the bar and watched the show, recalling the same antics from the Herc crew in Panama. It was a nearly identical situation, with Jake almost unable to keep the herd of drunken Coasties pointed towards the door. With a few last hollers, they all departed down the stairs and out onto George Street, leaving Cole alone with his thoughts.

He finally left, and outside, he took long breaths of the cold air and cleared his mind. He took one last walk down to the wharf before heading for Tony's. As he crossed a gravel lot to the street that paralleled the concrete wharf, he stopped and looked around, thinking for a moment that he'd lost his way. The *North Star* wasn't where she had been just a few hours before. Cole looked around at the warehouses and brick walls, convincing himself that he was in the right spot. As he stood there, it sank in. The boat was gone. *Shit,* he said to himself and started a brisk pace towards Tony's.

CHAPTER 10: EYES IN THE SKY

TONY DIDN'T PANIC when Cole broke the news. Rather, he asked Cole to start a pot of coffee while he disappeared into the upstairs room. Cole poured enough ground coffee into the basket to make it as thick as oil. He walked up the stairs and stopped a few feet from the open door. It was unusual for Tony to leave it open. He took a few more steps until Tony caught him in the corner of his eye. With a phone to his ear, he motioned for Cole to come in.

The room was a small space with a bright wooden floor. Tony had two tables and a laptop on each. Half a dozen chargers took up the bulk of one of the desktops. He was talking quietly into the phone, having just briefed up the development to some unseen command center. With a few nods, he hung up and turned to Cole.

"All right; we need to think."

Cole leaned against the doorframe casually and asked, "About what?"

Tony was bugged for a second but let go of it quickly. "How do we catch up to them? I haven't gotten any satellite imagery for at least two days. They could go anywhere."

Cole thought for a moment. "You're thinking Ireland, right?"

"Yeah; why?"

"I might know of a C-130 up here that could help."

Tony was silent, staring at Cole in something between disbelief and amazement. "How do you know that?"

"There's a Coast Guard Herc up here. I know the pilot. We were on a ship together."

Tony asked, "You mean *Delaney*?"

"Yup."

Tony shook his head and laughed. "Small world, huh?"

"Sure is."

"How do we find them?"

"I figure if we get to the airport around eight or so, we'll see them."

Tony countered, "It's a big airfield."

With a grin, Cole shot back, "It's a big-ass orange and white C-130. We'll find them."

Tony thought for a few moments more. "All right then. I've got some work to do in between. Is that coffee on?"

"Yeah. I'm gonna get some sleep if you don't mind. Wake me around six?"

"Will you sober up by then?"

Cole smiled. "Does it matter?"

They were out the door just after seven, driving for about 20 minutes before pulling up to the main terminal of the airport. Standing at a chain link fence, Cole scoured across the massive ramps and runways. Several smaller jets were taxiing and one or two 767s were swarmed with fuel trucks and power carts, prepping for flights later that morning. Tony looked off in the distance, craning his neck in search of the Herc. Seeing nothing, Cole walked about 50 yards to get a different angle. The ground arced up in the middle of the runway then sloped back down on the far side. Scanning the distance, he saw half a vertical stabilizer sticking up. It was white around the edges with the middle of it a bright and familiar orange shade of red. The building behind it had a yellow awning, but he couldn't make out much more.

"It's on the other side, Tony."

They hopped back in the truck and sped around to the far side. Back out on the main road, Tony found a side road leading to the general aviation and private ramps. Tony drove quickly, and Cole took it as a sign that he was growing impatient. They sped past some more warehouse-styled buildings then up one more side road before Cole spotted the awning.

"There, at the yellow building."

Tony parked, and they climbed up some wooden steps to the two glass doors. Once inside, a young and attractive girl looked up from behind a desk and smiled a friendly hello.

Cole walked up and leaned against the counter, asking, "Any chance the Coasties are around?"

"What did they do?"

Cole laughed. "No, it's not bad. I'm friends with the pilot."

She looked at him suspiciously before answering. "Well, most of them are outside getting ready, but I think one's still in the bathroom."

Tony was hanging back, letting Cole run the show. He walked over to the bathroom and opened the door, peering in but seeing nothing. Taking two more steps inside, he heard the familiar stomach surges of someone puking. A few more steps and he saw two black boots sticking out from the stall and a green flight suit around the guy's ankles. Cole waited for half a minute while the still-unknown dude let go of whatever was ailing him from the night before.

A few obligatory deep burps followed before the sound of a flushing toilet echoed in the cramped room. The man slowly stood and pulled up his flight suit and, stepping out of the stall, he zipped it back up. Casually, he wiped at his mouth and nodded at Cole before going over to the sink and running some water over his face.

Cole asked, "George Street?"

"Yeah, brother. Goddamn good time last night."

"Is Jake at the plane?"

The guy turned to Cole, stunned for a moment, and asked, "Who are you?"

"Just a friend. I need a favor from him."

The guy splashed some more water on his face then wiped it with a paper towel.

"All right." He paused and took a labored breath. "Follow me."

Back in the waiting room, Cole motioned for Tony to follow them. Outside another glass door, they followed around the plane and the guy lazily plugged both of his ears with his fingers as they rounded the nose of the plane and the scream from the APU grew louder. Up a set of crew stairs, the guy led Cole to the back of the plane where about 12 folks were standing around the back towards the ramp.

Jake saw him first. "Cole?"

"Hey, man. You got a minute?"

An older woman, also in a flight suit, cut in. "We're briefing a mission right now…"

Jake turned to her. "Commander, just a moment. I'll be right back."

He walked with Cole farther forward, past two pallets of toolboxes, cardboard boxes, survival suits, and some beat up sled-looking things.

Cole asked, "What is all this shit?"

Jake laughed. "What are you doing here?"

"I need a favor."

"What kind of favor?"

Cole looked at the sleds once more. "Seriously, what are those?"

Jake looked at him with disbelief. "Survival kits, in sleds in case we ditch on the ice."

Cole nodded and looked back at Jake who asked again, "Seriously, not the best time right now, Cole."

Cole pressed on. "This is my friend, Tony. Tony, this is Jake."

Tony extended his hand, "Nice to meet you, Jake."

From the back of the plane, the woman, by now clearly frustrated, loudly called out, "Lieutenant."

"Just a moment, Ma'am."

"Who is she?" Cole asked.

"Cole, for fuck's sake, what do you want?"

Tony opened his eyes wide and leaned forward, subtly begging Cole not to blow it.

"OK, yeah. So, can you find a boat for us?"

"Not right now. We're supposed to be doing ice reconnaissance."

"Are the icebergs going anywhere fast?"

Jake looked at him sternly. "No, Cole. They're not going fast. They're icebergs."

"Well, this boat is going faster, and it left a few hours ago. I just need you to find it, get a position, course, speed, you know—all the details."

Jake smirked. "What are you up to?"

"Nothing."

Tony chimed in. "Jake, I know you've got your tasking for today, and we're not trying to stop that, but if you can find this boat on your way out—they can't be more than a hundred miles from here right now, probably headed northeast."

Jake scratched his head and cleared his throat. "All right; we'll keep an eye out for it. You got a name?"

Cole and Tony spoke at the same time. "*North Star.*"

"Hmmm. Anything I should know about?"

Cole smiled. "Not right now, but maybe in a day or so. I'll find you guys downtown tonight?"

"Yeah. I'm sure we'll be there."

As Tony and Cole walked forward towards the cockpit, the same guy who'd puked in the bathroom was leaning against a bulkhead, his head leaning against a panel of circuit breakers with his eyes half closed. As Cole passed him, he patted him on the shoulder, "Hang in there, bud."

The guy smiled and nodded. Tony and Cole climbed down the stairs and back down to the asphalt ramp.

Over the whining scream of the APU, Tony asked, "You think they'll find her?"

Cole tapped on the turret that housed the camera on the front of the plane and looked over at Tony, "Yeah. They'll find her."

They hung around long enough to watch the C-130 lumber along down the taxiway to the far end of a runway. The sound of her engines groaning at full speed made Cole smile, and he watched in awe as the plane's nose lifted slowly off the ground and she climbed her way up into the chilly sky. The sound of the engines faded to a low rumble as she climbed up further through a level of thin clouds and disappeared.

Back at the house, Cole took a nap. After an hour or two, he took a shower and dressed a bit better than usual. There was no doubt Tony would notice, and when he did, he asked, "Meeting Olivia?"

"Leave it alone, Tony."

Tony laughed. "Have fun. Will you track down Jake later today?"

"Yeah. You want me to come back and grab you?"

Tony shook his head. "Nah. I'll be here when you get back. If it's late, wake me up."

"Will do."

With that, he was out the door and walked the Battery in the midday sun. It was cold but still, and Cole slowed so as not to sweat under his jacket. Twenty minutes later, he stepped inside the Duke of Duckworth. Olivia was seated at a small table by the wall. If she was happy to see him, she didn't show it. Then again, it was her style to leave a man guessing. She wore a thin green sweater and yet another shade of dark-red lipstick. Cole smiled before he knew it and tried to wipe it from his face to no avail.

He walked in and took a seat next to her. She leaned in and tilted her head, offering a simple hello.

"Hey there. You look good," Cole replied.

She said nothing back, but kept her eyes on his, resting her cheek against the back of her hand that was clasped in a loose fist with the other, her elbows resting on the table.

"I ordered you a Guinness."

"Perfect. We gonna eat?"

"If you'd like. The fish and chips are the best."

He nodded. "Fish and chips it is."

The waitress brought over Cole's beer, and Olivia took a sip of some whiskey drink before setting it down. They ordered a plate of fish and chips and the woman walked off, leaving Cole and Olivia to themselves. The bar was quiet with a handful of other patrons, most of whom were huddled around the bar on the far side of the room watching a curling match on the television. The bar was dark, as if there were laws in Newfoundland governing the amount of light allowed inside a drinking establishment. It wasn't run down, but it carried that kind of dive-bar vibe. Mismatched pictures were framed on the walls and random bits of memorabilia adorned the ledges.

Cole asked, "What color is your hair?"

"Why?"

"It always seems like it's a different shade depending on the room you're in."

"What color do you think it is?"

He sat back. "Well, it's not black and it's too dark to be brown. Sometimes it's got a hint of red."

"Is that all right with you?"

Cole paused as Olivia lifted her drink to her dark lips and took another sip. "I love it actually. Keeps me guessing."

She shifted in her seat and finally let her gaze wander somewhere else. When the food arrived, they'd shifted the conversation to Olivia's conflicting desire to travel the world and her love for Newfoundland. That, in turn, led to Cole letting on about little snippets of his life. They talked for the rest of the meal about the Caribbean. She was smart enough to know that his story was far too complex to not hide some underlying mischief.

"What were you doing down there?"

He looked at her. "Things I probably shouldn't have been doing."

"Is that why you're here?"

He took a breath and replied, "It's part of the reason."

The conversation hit a natural pause. She brushed strands of her hair back behind her ear then picked at a few more fries. Cole was done as well, and he settled the tab with cash when the waitress passed by.

"What now?"

She looked up and across the bar, then back at him. Her eyes had, for the time being, abandoned the wicked precision with which she sometimes skewered him. She looked at him with longing, as if she was about to ask him something. "I have something for you. Will you walk with me?"

"Sure."

They were out the door and set off up the sidewalk away from downtown. Five minutes later they were climbing a steep side street, the modest row houses painted in bright shades of green and blue and yellow, all of them well maintained.

"This is me."

She produced an oversized ring of keys and jiggled them until finding the right one. Cole followed her in and set his jacket down on a couch by the front door. In the small living room beside a tiny kitchen, Cole saw unfinished paintings and other bits of art in progress scattered about the room. He smiled at the little bit of added insight he now had about her.

"Is this yours?"

She looked at it for a moment and smiled. "Yeah. In my spare time."

She put down her jacket and kicked off her boots. Cole did the same, and she motioned him over to the stairs. She started up and turned to Cole, a sly smile sneaking out as she said softly, "Up here."

He was soon in her room and worked hard to slow his heartbeat. Her room smelled like a woman, and he stood next to her bed feeling awkward as she leaned into her closet and pulled out a soft and tattered leather case about the size of a purse. He thought that was what it was until she walked over, handed it to him, and he smelled the unmistakable scent of gun oil.

"Can I sit?"

"Sure," she said as they both sat down on the bed. Cole unzipped it and took a long breath when he set his eyes on the revolver inside. It was straight out of a western movie. A long octagonal barrel had an exposed rod underneath that pivoted into the chamber of the cylinder. Its trigger guard was made of brass, and a heavily oiled wooden grip and ornate hammer made up the rest of it.

Also in the case was a tarnished brass bell-shaped powder can and an old waxed paper bag of lead balls and some wool wads. A smaller tin container held several dozen percussion caps.

"Is this black powder?"

She shook her head and shrugged her shoulders. "I don't know. It was my grandfather's. I found it out in his shed. Is this what you were looking for?"

Cole smiled, unsure of how to respond. It was a far cry from the Glocks, M4s, or shotguns that he was accustomed to. It occurred to him that Harley would have most certainly thought it was awesome.

"Not exactly, but it'll do in a pinch. You don't mind if I borrow it?"

She shook her head, her hair again falling in front of her face. Cole set the gun aside on the nightstand and wiped his hands against his jeans. They were both silent for a moment, looking at each other for some direction. Olivia reached out with one hand and unfastened one button from his shirt. He didn't hesitate to reach over to her far leg and pull her quickly up and over his lap. She climbed on top of him, looking down with her face only inches from his. He held firm to her hips as they kissed and she worked at more of the buttons on his shirt.

His shirt off, he slid both his hands under her sweater, his palms against her pale bare skin and lifted it over her head. She locked both of her hands behind his neck and kissed him with some kind of unchecked passion he'd yet to see. Making quick work of her bra, he fell back onto her bed, Olivia on top of him as the rest of their clothes seemed to melt from their bodies. It was a raw kind of lust between them, and they fed off the shared passion like a wildfire. She was on top of him for some time, and when she lowered her chest down to rest on his, he wrapped his arms tight around and her pulled her closer. Both his fists were balled up and nearly trembling as he did his best to hold her with his forearms, unwilling to let go of the moment.

What followed was unpredictable waves of raw emotion tempered by tender lows as they each regained their breath and composure only to lose it as the next round of passion approached. They rolled and twisted to the far corners of her bed, and each time Cole thought that the sex might peak, Olivia would steady herself, slowing down with her eyes focused on his as they both rode down the back of a passing swell only to pick back up on the other side. He was entirely engrossed in her movements when they both finally shuddered, their bodies intertwined as the heavy breathing subsided, and each of them took longer-spaced breaths to slow their pulses. Cole was on his back with tiny beads of sweat across his chest, and Olivia was laid out next to him, one leg and one arm draped lazily over his body. He rested his hand on top of her arm and gripped it lightly.

"Stay here, with me, for a little while?" she asked.

He gripped her arm again. "I was hoping you might say that."

CHAPTER 11: THE OPEN SEA

HE DIDN'T WANT to leave, but as midnight approached, Cole reluctantly slid his boots on and gave Olivia one last kiss. She rolled over and stretched her arms outward, a thin sheet over her naked body that did little to mask her long and curved figure underneath. Cole took a long breath, laughing softly as he exhaled.

She bit her tongue and looked at him, her dark and dangerous eyes intently focused on his.

"Do you do that intentionally?"

"Do what?" she asked.

"With your eyes."

"What about them?"

Cole laughed. "Your eyes could break a man when they look that way."

She rolled and let her hair mask her face. From beneath the sheet, she reached upward, delicately tucking one strand behind her ear to reveal a sliver of her face. She was smiling again.

"I thought so," Cole said.

"Will you come by tomorrow?"

Cole looked at his watch to see it was already after midnight. "You mean today?"

"Whatever day it is. Come by tonight, then."

He nodded. "Yeah, I will."

Reaching over to the nightstand, he took the gun case and tucked it under one arm. Downstairs, he threw his jacket over his shoulders and tucked the gun inside, zipping up and cinching the jacket tight to hold it snug. The air was frigid outside, and he thought about Olivia's bed before shaking it from his mind. Jake and his crew would surely be downtown, and he was curious as to what they may have found.

It took him no more than half an hour to track down the crew at a hot-dog vendor on the side of George Street. Jake was eating an Italian sausage when Cole approached.

"You guys calling it quits?"

Jake shook his head. "Nah, just re-charging. We've got a few more hours in us."

Cole looked around at the handful of guys that were all in various stages of being happily drunk. Jake finished the last of his snack and asked, "You hungry?"

Cole shook his head and got down to the matter at hand, asking, "How'd today go?"

Jake deflected, almost as if he hadn't heard Cole. He turned to his crew, "Where to, boys?"

A chorus echoed out, "The Church, Sir."

Jake shook his head, but they persisted. "Just one drink, Sir, then we'll get back to it."

Cole watched to see Jake's reaction.

"Fuck it, one drink."

The crew cheered, and they made their way farther to the end of George Street. 'The Church,' as it was known, had actually been a church at some point in its long and sordid history. Nowadays, it was a gentlemen's club on a good day and a den of debauchery on a bad one. Some of Jake's crew were more eager than the others and they scurried up the stairs towards the pulsing blue and red lights on the second floor. Cole paid Jake's cover and the two walked up, around a corner, and to the bar. Cole tucked his jacket—and the canvas bag inside of it—on a seat by the wall where he could keep an eye on it. Inside, the high ceiling still bore some resemblance to a house of worship. Several of Jake's crew were already up front worshipping and offering penance, one dollar at a time. Jake bought a round of beers, and the two settled onto stools. Shitty dance music blared over the speakers as a better-than-average girl made her rounds up on the stage. Cole's curiosity was interrupted when Jake finally put his beer down and spoke.

"We found the *North Star*."

Cole turned to face him, not entirely surprised, and asked, "Where?"

"I'd guess they're heading for Ireland, like you said. No more than one hundred miles out. No fishing gear on deck; they're just steaming."

"Could you find them tomorrow?"

Jake shook his head. "Doubt it. We're flying up through the Straits of Belle Isle, not really in their direction."

Two from his crew stumbled past with their hands full of fresh bottles and made their way back up towards the stage as a second girl stepped up and began her routine on what must have been a 20-foot pole. The first girl was now sitting with the guys and making herself richer by the second.

"How long are you guys up here for?"

Jake took a long sip to finish his beer. "Through the end of next week."

"Every night like this?"

Jake grinned. "Yup."

"Maybe I should've been a pilot."

Jake laughed and started to stand to grab another round before Cole pushed down on his shoulder and stood himself. "I got this one."

The floor was crowded now with the early morning gathering of drunks, both visitors and locals alike, who stumbled over top of each other to secure some one-on-one time with any of the dozen or so girls wandering the bar. Armed with two more Stellas, Cole returned to his seat and looked towards the main floor to see that one of Jake's crew was now being led up on stage, much to the amusement of the rest of them.

Two girls made quick work of the young guy, laying him down on his back and dancing over top of him. A minute later, they rolled him over to his stomach and lightly spanked him a few times, looking to his friends for encouragement. The whole bar was now watching and offering vile yet amusing words to egg them on. They both spanked him a few more times, and his comrades seated close by threw more and more money on stage until one of the girls took off his belt and held it up for the whole establishment to see. At the behest of his friends and the rest of the bar, the second girl tugged at his jeans until they were down around knees, leaving only his boxers around his waist. He was laughing and shaking his head, unable to stop whatever was happening over the top of him.

The two girls spanked him lightly again as the bar began to chant. The energy grew and Cole laughed, leaning over to Jake. "I don't think this is going to end well."

Jake took a long sip, finishing half his beer before wiping at his lip. "Nope, probably not." Even Jake was mesmerized by it.

A moment later, one girl straddled the guy's legs and ripped at his boxers, exposing his bare white ass. With precision, the girl standing with the belt let it fly and smacked his ass with a vigorous and almost alarming level of energy. He winced in pain as his buddies howled with laugher. Given the vulnerable circumstances, he tried to mask whatever fear was now likely running through his mind. She struck again and he arched his back, the pain visible on his face.

She passed the belt to the other girl who unleashed a series of blows against his now-rosy ass. He tried to get up, but neither girl was finished with him, and they were doing a good job of keeping him pinned down. Like the dramatic death of a gladiator at the Roman Coliseum, a chorus of approval echoed throughout the main floor. The first girl took the belt back and struck him even harder.

"Holy fuck," Cole said with an uncertain combination of fascination and fear on his face.

Jake spoke plainly. "That's gonna hurt in the morning."

"Who is he?"

"Good dude. He's one of the Mission System Operators, works the radar and camera."

Cole nodded. "Assuming he can manage to sit tomorrow."

One girl whipped him again.

"Or today."

The other took a turn and the snap of the leather on his skin caused both Cole and Jake to wince.

"Good point."

They both finished their beers. As the ladies finished up, they helped the guy get his jeans back on and returned his belt. They even both gave him kisses. In his drunken stupor, he likely didn't feel much of it anyhow as he clumsily staggered back down to where the rest of his crew was seated. Slowly, the club returned to its normal pace of operations, and as the two masochistic girls made their post-routine rounds, they were greeted with high-fives and smiles by the drunken horde.

"Cole asked, "What time y'all start tomorrow?"

"0800."

"You know it's past two in the morning?"

Jake looked at his watch and smirked. "Yeah. Might get these boys to bed."

Tony worked things from his end, and somehow he managed to track the *North Star*'s rendezvous with an Irish coastal fishing boat about 20 miles off the west coast of Ireland. With the *North Star* steaming back for Newfoundland, the small shipment was quickly interdicted once it hit the docks. It was a small win, but as Tony explained, it turned up the pressure on the whole operation, and that was in itself the greatest victory.

A week had passed without much action in St. John's. Cole sat in the living room with Tony, both of them sipping coffee and playing hypotheticals back and forth. Carl was involved, and both of them were now certain that he was using his position to his advantage to keep the operation moving unhindered.

"I just don't know why he's doing it."

Tony took a short sip. "Money."

Cole rubbed his chin, three days' worth of stubble like sandpaper against his fingers. "I'm not convinced. He's got some ulterior motive."

"I've been doing this a while. It's almost always money. If not that, it's power."

Cole asked, "Power over what? You think he's gonna run for mayor or something?"

Tony laughed. "I don't see him as the political type."

Cole, his hand still pressed against his face, scratched his jaw and turned his neck until it cracked. His thoughts turned to Olivia. For a moment, they wandered across the Atlantic to Isabella and Marie, then with a deep breath he brought them back to his present surroundings.

"Where's the boat now?"

Tony shook his head. "Dunno, no satellites."

"Can we put a tracker on it?"

"Piece of cake, but it'd be nice to know when they're coming back in. If they're carrying drugs back again, we could ratchet it up some more with Carl."

"My buddy is still in town. Wanna commandeer that Herc?"

Tony laughed. "You think we could?"

"I think you could."

They both paused, a laughable silence overcoming both of them. Tony took a long breath. "I don't want to play that card just yet. You think he'd be willing to take a look for us again?"

Cole nodded and set his empty coffee mug down. "Yeah. I'll find him tonight and ask."

———

By midnight, Cole had spotted two of Jake's guys stumbling with the masses down George Street. He followed them into the Martini Bar where the rest of the crew was huddled around a back table. Playing up the image of a more upscale drinking establishment, the Martini Bar lacked the old wooden décor and tried to fit in with the chic and trendy bars of a more urban setting. It was a magnet for the cougars of downtown St. John's, and several of Jake's guys were slowly being ensnared by a few of the more agile women. They seemed to not mind at all.

Jake and Cole took a seat near the back of the bar, against the windows overlooking George Street, and each nursed a rum and Coke done up in a fancy glass.

"Can you look for that boat again tomorrow?"

Jake nodded. "Yeah, we'll be northeast again. But I want to know what I'm looking for."

Cole took a long breath. "They're moving stuff, maybe drugs, maybe guns—we don't really know."

"Who is that dude you're staying with?"

"Tony?"

Jake smiled. "Yeah. Who is he working for?"

"You trying to get a medal or something?" joked Cole.

"Fuck you." They both laughed.

Cole said, "I honestly don't know who he works for, never have, and don't really care. But he's good shit."

Jake looked around the bar then shifted his focus back to his drink, and with some seeming regret, said, "We're leaving a day after tomorrow."

Cole thought for a moment and asked, "And the next crew?"

"The aircraft commander is a tool. Probably not gonna give you the time of day."

"What about you? Are you coming back?"

Jake nodded. "Yeah. I'll give the liver a few weeks to recover and be back up middle of next month."

"That's good."

He asked, "Why's that?"

"May need you."

The conversation turned to a lighter topic as one of Jake's guys walked arm in arm with a blonde who was in all likelihood in her late

30s. Jake's guy was no more than 30, and he tossed a devilish grin at both Cole and Jake as they walked out the door.

"Man down, huh?"

Jake laughed. "He'll be just fine."

"So what about you? You above all of this or what?" asked Cole.

Jake grinned, holding something back.

Cole pressed the issue. "What's that grin all about?"

"I've got a lady up here, little bit older than me. We get together from time to time."

Cole nodded. "That simple, huh?"

"I wish it was simple. We met a few years back and seem to keep linking up when I'm in town."

"Where's she tonight?"

"Probably with her fiancé."

Cole almost choked on the fizzle of rum and Coke in his mouth. He swallowed and chewed on his lip for a moment. "Jesus, that sounds complicated."

"Yeah, not so simple, huh?"

"So why are you keeping at it?"

Jake held up his glass to the bartender and motioned for two more.

"Blue eyes and black hair, man. It does something to me."

Cole paused for a moment and spoke. "There's something in the water up here, huh?"

They finished their round of drinks and parted ways, Cole having been overcome by a desire to see what Olivia was up to. They promised to meet up the following night, when Jake would hopefully have an update on the *North Star*.

Strolling down the dark stairwell to the UnderBelly, he grinned when Olivia looked his way.

Taking a seat, he said, "Hey, darling."

She replied with a devastating combo, her eyes looking right through his and a strand of hair falling casually in front of her face. She said nothing, but poured him a stout and brought it over as if she knew with certainty the way Cole felt about her. Leaning in, they kissed each other's cheeks and she went back to pouring a round of beers. The crowd was in good spirits, time having washed away much of the immediate pain of the past few weeks.

When she returned, she asked, "You haven't been robbing any banks, have you?"

"Huh?"

She tilted her head and explained the rest with her eyes.

The gun, he thought.

"No, no. It's tucked away in my room."

"I'm off in two hours. You sticking around?"

He grinned at her. "Probably best if I walk you home, huh?"

Olivia smiled then looked down, as if she was about to blush. Before she could, she recovered and leaned against the bar, close to Cole. He felt some kind of normalcy in their relationship, where the silence was no longer uncomfortable and the two of them could just be together, even if on other sides of the bar, and things were as they should be.

He asked, "You got plans tomorrow?"

She turned to him, shaking her head, unsure as to where his question was going. "No. Why?"

"No reason. Might be nice to sleep in, though."

"So you're staying the night now?"

He looked first around the bar then quickly back to her. "Yeah, if you'll let me."

CHAPTER 12: TIGHTEN THE NOOSE

HE WOKE UP IN Olivia's room, the faintest scent of a flower wafting through the air. On his side, he reached behind his back and felt her side. She stirred to let him know she was awake. He didn't hesitate to roll over, halfway on top of her, and brush her hair out of her face. Before she could even smile, he was kissing her. A long drawn-out moan told him she didn't object, and they pressed against each other, the first spark of a wildfire between the two of them. She matched his raw emotion as they fed off of each other and shook away the stillness of an otherwise calm morning.

When they finished, Cole wiped sweat from his forehead and laughed as he caught his breath. As Olivia's head sunk back into her pillow, she asked, "What got into you?"

"Nothing. Just felt like feeling you again."

She exhaled loudly, rolled to Cole's side, and ran her bare foot up and down the side of his leg.

"Breakfast?"

She looked at him. "Sure. Here or out?"

"Let's go out."

"Do you have to do anything today?"

Cole shook his head. "No, not until tonight."

"OK, let me get some clothes on."

As she stood up, Cole stayed in her bed and admired Olivia's naked body as she casually walked around her room. Whatever emotional process he'd gone through over the past year or so, he felt as if he'd reached a healing point. Isabella had made it clear where their relationship stood and Cole felt, for the first time in a long time, no guilt for seeking out the affections of another woman. He knew too that Isabella deep down wanted him to be happy. He wondered for a moment if she too had moved on. The emotional connection that had haunted him for so long was broken, and Cole was relieved. Olivia was wild too, his thoughts going back to her grabbing at his hair when they were in bed and making no attempt to keep her passion in check.

"What are you grinning at?"

He snapped back to the moment at hand. Olivia stood near the window, backlit from the morning light, and Cole could just faintly make out the green lace of her panties that she'd pulled on.

"Come here," he said. He reached out and took Olivia's hands, pulling her on top of him. She straddled his waist and lowered her face down to his, her hair tickling his neck as it fell from behind her ears.

Surprised, she asked, "Again?"

———

Breakfast turned into lunch at a coffee shop. Afterwards, the afternoon idled away and they talked casually until Olivia had to get herself ready for work. He kissed her cheek, watched her walk away, and then made his way back to Tony's. Walking inside, Cole tossed his coat down on the couch and took a seat. Tony emerged from upstairs and asked, "You good?"

Cole kicked off his boots, "I'm good."

"Any luck with Jake?"

Cole, now laying down, his arms up and crossed behind his head, replied, "Yup. I'll link up with him tonight."

"How's Olivia?"

Cole looked up as Tony walked past him towards the kitchen. "She's good."

From the kitchen, Tony asked, "And you?"

"I'm good, man." He paused and thought, then continued with a smile. "Yeah, I'm good."

———

Cole found Jake that evening, and the two found a quiet corner of the bar at Shamrock City. Tony joined them later and the three huddled up close while Jake showed them some photos he'd transferred to his phone. The *North Star* had a clean deck, no fishing gear to be seen, and was steaming back for St. John's at 12 knots. Jake had a photo with a time stamp that gave Tony a good enough position to dead reckon when they'd reach the coast.

He excused himself to make a phone call, leaving Jake and Cole to themselves.

"So what is it carrying?"

Cole replied, "Probably drugs."

He looked at Jake and smiled. "I mean it, though—you can't say shit to anyone about this."

"Got it."

"I mean it, dude. You don't want to get yourself roped into this stuff."

Jake nodded, looked towards the door, and smiled. Cole turned to see a woman in her late 30s. Her hair was jet black and even from across the bar, Cole could see her blue eyes as they looked at him before turning to Jake. She smiled and made her way over to their corner.

"That's her, huh?"

Jake grinned. "Yup. She'll be the death of me." Jake stood up and gave her a hug and a sly kiss on her cheek.

"Cole, this is Carol."

"Nice to meet you," Cole said.

She smiled back at him, not certain if she liked him or not.

Jake cut in, "Cole and I have known each other for a long time. We were on a ship together years ago."

She seemed more comfortable at that and took a seat in between the two of them.

Jake asked, "Drinks?"

They ordered a round, Jake and Cole opting for Guinness while Carol ordered a gin and tonic. She was gorgeous in the kind of seductive way that the women of Newfoundland had mastered over the centuries—delicate enough to tease a man incessantly, but equally as capable of breaking them in half. Men had, since the early days of wooden ships, spent their fortunes on drinks for the ladies of St. John's only to wake up and be forced to sea again to recoup their losses while the women slept away their hangovers in the comfort of their own beds.

Carol asked, "So what brings you to St. John's, Cole?"

"I'm staying with a friend for a bit. I needed a break from the States."

She toyed with her drink and Cole looked away to avoid being drawn in by her deep blue eyes. He looked to Jake, who only grinned, and from behind Carol he shrugged his shoulders as if to concede defeat once more. They both took long sips from their beer and feigned interest in the opening act up on stage. He played some American country cover songs as the bar worked its way into the nightly rhythm.

Carol whispered something to Jake and he nodded. A moment later, Carol herself took a long sip, nearly draining her glass. Jake too seemed to hurry up with his. Cole understood that he'd be left alone in a matter of minutes. He couldn't help but be drawn in by Carol. She turned to him and asked, "So, are you still in the Coast Guard?"

He shook his head.

She paused, waiting for him to explain. With a grin, he continued, "I was, for a few years, but it didn't work out."

"So what do you do now?"

"A little bit of everything."

She finished her drink with one last sip and replied with a simple uninterested nod. "Hmmm."

Turning to Jake, she must have said something with her eyes, as he took one last swig from his pint, set the glass down and looked at Cole. "We're gonna head out for a bit."

Standing up, Carol shifted out of the way, and Cole gripped Jake's hand firmly, pulling him into a hug. "Damn good to see you, man."

"We're leaving in the morning. Sorry I couldn't stay longer."

"All good," Cole said.

Jake held Cole's grip. "I'm back up early next month if you need anything."

Cole nodded. "Yeah, I may lean on ya again."

"Anything, brother. You just ask."

Carol and Jake made for the door, passing Tony as he walked back in. He looked quizzically at Jake for a moment, who must have smiled a shit-eating grin as they passed, because Tony looked confused when he joined Cole at the bar. "Who was that?"

"It's complicated," Cole said.

"You guys are all a shit show. Every fucking last one of you."

Cole smiled. "Who?"

Tony, shaking his head, replied, "Coasties."

Cole laughed out loud. "I won't argue that one."

He ordered another beer, and Tony motioned with two fingers for one as well. Surprised, Cole asked, "You celebrating or something?"

Tony grinned. "Yeah. I talked with the governor. The Canadian Coast Guard is getting underway in the next hour or so. They're gonna intercept the *North Star*."

"So now what?"

"We need to find Carl," Tony said with a smile.

———

The following morning, Cole and Tony watched from a crowd downtown as the Coast Guard ship offloaded the four men from the *North Star*, each of them handcuffed, to a waiting police van. Cameras from Canadian news channels were rolling then as the governor stood next to several customs agents who held gallon-sized bags of colored pills.

He made a quick speech, thanking the Coast Guard and Customs agents, then hammered home his intolerance for the illicit trade. Underneath was a politically charged tone, but the governor seemed to balance it well. Cole was busy trying to dissect the governor's true agenda when Tony bumped him on the shoulder. He nodded towards the side, where Cole could see Carl standing in the background of the side of the small gathering. He was clearly trying to hide his frustration. In all likelihood, it was only Tony and Cole who knew the depth of Carl's involvement. Perhaps the governor had his suspicions, but he'd remained quiet about them in conversation with Tony.

A moment later, Carl locked his eyes on the two of them. Tony nodded and Cole stared back expressionless. The governor wrapped up his comments then turned the microphone over to the Customs Chief who took a few questions and dodged answers about how they'd found the boat or known about its purpose. As the crowd dispersed and the camera crews broke down their gear, Tony and Cole walked over to Carl who was standing by himself, his hands dug deep into the pockets of his winter jacket.

"Big win, huh?"

Carl stared at Tony for a second. "Sure is. You have anything to do with it?"

"Can't say that I did, and you?"

Carl shook his head, looking away as he spoke. "No, not on my end."

He took a long breath and looked out over the harbor. The sky was blueish grey, a thin layer of clouds masking the contour of the sun that was high in the noontime sky. Carl was fidgeting, and Tony backed off so as not to push him too far.

"Any progress with the warehouse?"

Carl looked at Cole. "No. They're all still dead if that's what you're asking."

"I meant with where the drugs came from."

Carl cleared his throat. "We're still looking at it. You got anything you want to tell me?"

Cole smiled. "Me? No, just glad you all were able to stop it from happening again."

He grunted with a low voice. "Yeah."

Silence followed, and Carl turned to look down the length of the wharf. He looked back to the two of them and nodded. "I should be going. Stay in touch. If you hear anything, I'd like to know."

Tony waved with two fingers. "You got it, Carl."

As he walked away, Cole and Tony watched him, walking quickly and scanning occasionally up to the town or down at the boats.

"He's dirty as fuck."

Tony asked, "Is that a technical term?"

A smile formed on one side of Cole's mouth. "Yeah."

As the two of them walked back to the Battery, a dark sedan with tinted windows was waiting in the driveway. When they approached, the back window came down and the governor smiled from inside.

Tony asked, "Sir, how are you?"

"I'm good. Just wanted to say thanks to you both."

"Our pleasure, Sir."

He looked at Cole for a second, doing a doubletake with his face unable to hide his uncertainty. "I hope you'll keep me in the loop as this thing progresses."

Tony nodded. "Yes, Sir. We will."

"Great, great. If there's anything from my end that you need, please don't hesitate to ask."

He looked at Cole again, then rolled up the window and motioned for his driver to go. The car pulled slowly out of the driveway and turned for town. Cole and Tony walked inside.

Cole asked, "So what now?"

"We turn the screws on Carl, keep an eye on him."

"You think he'll make a move again?"

Tony, taking a seat by the large window, nodded. "Yeah, I think he's in a world of shit now. If he's calling the shots on any of this, he's lost a shipment of guns and now a shipment of drugs, too. Someone is going to recoup their losses one way or the other."

"You want me to keep an eye on the waterfront?"

"That'd be a good start."

Cole nodded, knowing that the next few weeks may hold long nights. He made his way back to his room to catch some sleep.

———※———

As midnight approached, he was seated at the same bar overlooking the center wharf. A half-dozen fishing boats were tied up as a light mist fell outside. Cole nursed a Guinness for the better part of an hour before he reluctantly finished it and ordered a second. He was quick with the beer, and as the bar wound down for the evening, he made his way outside and sat on a pile of pallets under the shadows of a soaked brick wall. It afforded him an unobstructed view of most of the boats. He'd focused in on one that had shown some activity an hour prior.

In the wheelhouse, a light was intermittently on and off for the better part of an hour. By now, Cole knew what to look for. He pulled his jacket up around his cheeks and dug his hands in deep. On his left side, he felt the outline of the pistol. The belt draped over his right shoulder, the holster sitting comfortably under his armpit. After waking up from his nap that afternoon, he'd painstakingly loaded it, pouring powder carefully into each chamber, plugging them with wads of wool, then seating the lead balls and crushing percussion caps against the nipples on the outside of the cylinder. If the gun even worked. Cole had no idea. But all things considered, the pistol was in excellent shape, and Cole wondered about Olivia's grandfather and what things the man had seen or done with the gun.

He pulled his right hand out of his pocket, running his fingers together to shake the chill, then reached through his jacket to feel the wooden grip protruding from under his arm. In his jacket, it was dry, but Cole wondered what would happen if the caps were to get wet from the incessant cold mist that hung in the nighttime air. By two in the morning, Cole was shivering every few minutes. Under his jacket, his torso was dry, but his pants were now damp despite his best effort to shield himself from the persistent moisture. He would give it another hour or so then make his way back to Tony's. If nothing happened by three in the morning, he reckoned the night was a bust.

As he sniffled and wiped at his nose, he heard the tires of a car coming up from behind him on the wharf. As expected, it pulled up close to the boat that Cole had fixated on. The light came back on inside the wheelhouse, and two men emerged from the car. As they did, a second van pulled up behind it, and another figure stepped out from the driver's side. Cole didn't move a single muscle. He was no more than 50 yards from them and could hear bits and pieces of their muffled conversation.

From the trunk of the car, one man grabbed two duffel bags and tossed them onto the deck of the boat. At the back of the van, two men were offloading cases. They were rifle-length and heavy by the looks of it. All of the men moved quickly and within two minutes, one man climbed over the gunwale onto the boat, a second man got back in the driver's seat of the car, and the last man, looking more and more like Carl, hung back on the wharf, discussing something with the two of them now standing on the deck of the boat.

As he finally got back in the van and began to drive off, Cole watched as one of the guys on the boat cast off the stern line and worked his way to the bow. Sure enough, the hum of the old diesel engine came to life as the guy tossed the bow line back onto the wharf. *Shit*, Cole thought. He heard her spool up as the old engine stumbled, then caught its rhythm. Cole took a long breath. The guy on deck cast off the third of four lines, leaving only a spring line just aft of the wheelhouse. As the guy walked into the wheelhouse, the deck was empty, and Cole chewed at the side of his mouth, then hopped up, ducked low, and ran the 30 yards across the vacant lot. Now crouched down by a large bit on the wharf, he watched as the boat backed down on the last line and the bow lazily swung around into the harbor. The guy on deck tossed the last line back and walked forward into the wheelhouse. Cole heard the engine crank, reversing the propeller to clutch ahead as the boat gained momentum. He swallowed, but his mouth was dry. *Fuck*, he thought as he looked back across the empty wharf. Standing, he sprinted the last ten yards, jumped off the wharf, over the transom and down to the deck, clinging to a low pile of traps on the stern of the boat.

HIS HAIR WAS matted down, cold water running from his forehead, down his nose, and soaking the shirt underneath his jacket. Sitting back low against the transom, Cole looked aft to see the wharf fading away behind him. There was no light above him, not from the moon nor from a single star as a low overcast haze hung over the North Atlantic sky. To the east, the mouth of the harbor was barely visible as the old boat lumbered on.

He poked his head around the pile of traps to see that the hatch into the wheelhouse was open. Whomever was at the helm cast a shadow down on the deck from a solitary green light inside. The second crewmember emerged and Cole crouched low, ducking back into the darkness. Against the port side, the gruff young man picked up two bags, straining with the weight of them, and carried them inside. They were rifles, of that Cole was quite certain as all the evidence pointed to another run, no doubt hastily put together by Carl to balance out his losses. There were six more bags against the railing, and Cole waited patiently as the guy came back three more times and carried them all inside.

They were now in the middle of the harbor, steaming at around six knots for the mouth and beyond to the open Atlantic. Cole could see the opposing cliffs under the palest of blue light, the features of the rocks indistinguishable from under the fingers of icy snow that clung to them. He turned to look back, second guessing himself as he realized his options were running out. Without Jake to watch from above, if the boat made it past the harbor without Tony noticing, they were more or less home free.

Cole took a long breath, the sea and the exhaust stinging his nostrils. It calmed him enough that his pulse steadied. Here he was, yet again, in uncharted territory. Tony would certainly not approve of his being on the boat, nor would he condone any of the ideas that Cole was considering. Then again, Cole had never been guided by anyone's intentions other than his own. He wiped a sheen of cold water from his face and tried to dry his hands on his jeans, but they were now soaked from the mist that had turned to a light rain. Reaching inside his jacket, he felt once more for the wooden grip of his pistol.

The mouth of the harbor was quickly approaching. To his left, he saw the Battery approaching and all at once wished that he was dry, warm, and seated at the couch looking out over the cold and dark entrance to the harbor. *Focus*, he told himself. He unzipped the jacket halfway and drew the pistol with his right hand, cupping the hammer and cylinder with his left hand to keep the percussion caps dry. He squeezed the wooden grips and aligned his hand for a comfortable hold. It felt natural and strong, having been almost a year since he'd last held a gun. Despite the added confidence, Cole knew too well the odds of a gunfight.

Stepping around the traps, he watched in silence for half a minute to be certain that both of them were in the wheelhouse. Counting shadows, he stepped up to the hatch and peered inside. It smelled of cigarette smoke and fish, the faintest trace of diesel doing little to mask the years of honest work now marred by an illicit run. Perhaps it wasn't their first trip like this, perhaps it was. Cole knew that he'd likely kill both of them. It was too far-fetched of an idea that he could scare them straight or even send any kind of message. The Battery was now directly to his left, the open Atlantic a mere 300 yards away. He took a long breath, held it in his lungs for a moment, then exhaled and stepped inside.

"What's the plan, boys?"

As he asked, he cocked the hammer and held the gun at a low draw. They both turned to Cole and neither said a word.

"What's in the bags?"

They looked at each other for a moment, then back at Cole. The rattling of the engine shook the deck as none of them said a thing to break the tension.

The one not at the wheel, a lean but strong looking young guy, lunged at Cole. Mid-step, Cole touched the trigger and surprised even himself as the hammer dropped and an explosion of sparks flew from the cylinder and muzzle. The cabin was clouded in smoke and Cole dropped to one knee, confirming that he'd hit the guy low in his gut. It wasn't a kill shot, rather it was the kind that would lead to a slow agonizing death. He'd aimed higher, or so Cole thought. Doubled over on the deck, the guy was moaning in pain and clutching his stomach as blood stained his shirt and pants. Cole stood again and kicked him over to his side, cocking the hammer once more in a fluid motion as he pointed the pistol at the second guy. The smoke had lifted to the ceiling where it swirled with the wind that snuck in from an open porthole.

Cole stepped farther forward and drove his knee into the neck of the one he'd hit to keep him pinned on the deck.

"What did Carl tell you?"

The one who was shot was now bleeding profusely through his shirt. Cole looked at the one at the wheel and asked once more, "What did Carl tell you?"

The guy at the helm, a bit thicker than the first with an unkempt reddish beard, looked forward at the mouth of the harbor, at Cole, then forward again.

"Carl's not here to help you."

The guy on the deck moaned again and tried to move, but couldn't under the weight of Cole's knee. They were fast approaching the mouth and Cole aimed low, taking out the guy's shin with another shot. He didn't fall, but lifted his left and fell against the side of the cabin, catching himself with both hands.

Steadying himself, he was understandably mad and yelled, "What the fuck are you doing?"

Cole cocked the hammer a third time and pointed it at his good leg.

The guy screamed, spit flying from his mouth as he did, "We're headed for the coast of Ireland. That's all I know."

"Bullshit," Cole yelled.

He pressed his knee further into the guy's neck to press him. "What about you? You want me to let you go?"

The guy, clenching both his fists against his stomach, was now sweating profusely and seemed close to giving in. Cole reared back and popped him on his head with the muzzle of the gun, cutting a small slice of skin open over his temple.

"You want to live?"

He was about to speak, then stopped, the last bit of resolve almost but not quite gone from his busted body.

"Guns or drugs?"

The guy driving spoke first. "We're dropping the guns off first, then picking up some packages to bring back. That's all I know."

"So the drugs are coming from Ireland?"

"I don't fucking know where they're coming from. We're just picking them up."

"Who gets the guns?"

The guy at the wheel steadied himself again and shifted his weight on his remaining good leg. His other was covered in blood that was now pooling on the bare wooden deck.

"None of my business who gets them."

Cole looked down to the one he was leaning on, and they made eye contact. Cole squinted and stared at him, pressing the muzzle against the guy's head. As he did, he caught the other guy moving and looked up to see that he'd grabbed a filet knife. Cole touched off a third shot, catching the guy squarely in the chest. He fell to his side, landing on his left shoulder, the details of his mortal wound obscured by the lingering smoke. His lifeless eyes were still open and no more than a foot from Cole as he leaned further into the first guy's neck. He was panicked at the death of his friend, and Cole eased up the pressure on his neck. The guy took a long, labored breath then looked at Cole. He'd lost any fight left in him.

Cole asked, "How many times have you made this run?"

The guy said nothing.

Cole was now calm and almost regretful. He hoped the guy was a criminal and not some local fisherman drawn into a bad crowd for the first time.

"Do you know the guys who got caught the other day?"

He nodded.

Cole asked, "Friends of yours?"

The guy shifted for a moment to relieve some of the pain. "My cousin."

"How many boats are doing this?"

The guy took a short and labored breath, but said nothing.

Cole asked calmly, "How many boats?"

"It's just been the two of us. My uncle and Carl go back a ways."

"Who is your uncle?"

"He was the captain on the *North Star*."

"So now it's just the two of you?"

"We didn't want to do it, but Carl squeezed us pretty good."

Cole thought for a moment, then asked, "How many runs have you done?"

The guy groaned for a moment. "Maybe six."

It was enough to satisfy Cole. He stood up, and the two of them stared at each other in silence. Cole cocked the hammer once more and finished the guy off with a fourth shot. His ears were ringing and the details of the cabin, its cramped and messy console, worn wooden wheel and torn seats, were veiled by a thin stagnant layer of smoke from the black powder. He lowered the pistol to his side and stood for a moment as the boat steamed on. Out the side windows, he could see the sheer cliffs as the boat passed the narrowest section.

Fuck, he told himself, and took one last look at the two dead men lying at his feet. Blood ran from their wounds and soaked a matted dirty green carpet against the aft area of the wheelhouse. The smoke persisted still, and Cole took a long breath as it mixed with the traces of a smoldering cigarette that would now go to waste. He wiped at his nose and turned unceremoniously to walk out, stuffing the pistol back in its holster as he stepped outside.

Peering around the bridge, he could see the open Atlantic a mere hundred yards farther along. The trawler steamed along, her course steady despite a dead crew. Cole looked up at the cliffs that towered over him to the north, moonlight piercing the now-heavy cold rain that came down harder and harder.

One day, he told himself. *One day I'll think these things through.*

He thought about heading back to the wheelhouse and turning the boat closer to the rocks, but if it foundered now, he'd have to explain himself. *Fuck me.* He threw one leg over the gunwale, then the second, and pushed off the narrow railing away from the hull and into the water. He knew from his time racing sailboats in the Northeast that cold water induced immediate shock. He also knew that mentally one could push through it, at least for a short period of time.

It sucked the breath out of him and as he submerged momentarily, Cole fought his body as it tried to inhale. The hull bumped him hard as it passed, and he kicked to the surface away from her to take a labored breath as his body shivered uncontrollably. Turning his head, he saw the fishing boat slowly steaming along, towards a bank of fog that hugged the coastline. Back to his left, he knew within a few seconds that the current was ripping out to sea with the ebbing tide. The mouth was a chokepoint, and he could see the individual rocks drifting off to his right. Against a concrete cube on which was mounted a small navigation beacon, Cole saw the whitewater reflecting in the moonlight and he kicked once more, clawing at the water with all his strength.

His fingers were already numb, his boots doing little to propel him forward as he kicked in vain. He dared not stop to shed his boots or his clothes, resigning himself to use only his arms to make any headway towards the rocks. As the current pulled him further along to the open sea, he tried to measure his forward progress against the lateral drift that sucked him towards a certain death. Small ripples were enough to sting his face as he tried to keep his mouth above the water. With each bit of water against his cheeks, he felt his mouth numbing and even clenching his lips shut became increasingly difficult.

Despite his effort, Cole could feel the numbness climbing up his extremities. He thought for a moment back to the Coast Guard Academy where instructors had taught him to tie knots underwater in a bucket of ice water. As the cadets' fingers lost any sensation, the instructors drove home the reality of what cold water could do. He took some comfort in the recollection that he'd successfully tied Bowline knots until the instructors finally relented and let them take their hands out of the buckets. Cole had been the only one who persisted.

He clawed again at the water, fully aware of his desperate state. To his right, there was a low pile of boulders and he dead reckoned that he might make it. Another minute passed before he felt a large flat rock under his feet. He was unable to stand on it as the chest deep water carried him off of it and towards another. Swimming still, Cole clung to the next one that he found and pulled himself to shallower water. He rested for a moment and turned back towards the open Atlantic as the boat's stern disappeared, now little more than a ghost in the fog.

Resting was not an option. His feet were numb, the absence of any tread on his boots making it even more difficult to get his footing on the thick fingers of seaweed that clung to the surface of the submerged stone. He pulled with his forearms wrapped around the man-sized rocks until he was completely out of the water. He shed his jacket, tucking the pistol and its holster in a crevice between two larger rocks. From there, he clawed his way up, slipping along the way as he made his way up the precarious face of the cliff.

Thankfully, there was a path of sorts that led him to the top, where he found the narrow gravel trail leading back to the Battery. His wet boots slid and slipped as he walked, his arms curled up to his chest and his fingers entirely useless. Fifty yards into it, he fell from exhaustion, landing hard on a pile of rocks. Laying on the wet gravel, he shivered and wondered for a brief second if he could get back up. Gritting his teeth, he willed himself up and to his knees before almost falling again.

Finally up and walking, he took great comfort in the sight of the wooden deck that marked the entrance to the trail. It was a halfway point. Once on the pavement, he was able to move quicker. Trying in vain to run, he nearly fell again and resigned to walking. He almost laughed as his stride was that of a drunken sailor stumbling off George Street. At best, his legs could only wobble underneath him. Continuing on past the neatly spaced houses, he shivered violently and side-stepped to his right as his right leg nearly gave out on him. He leaned for a few seconds against a low fence and caught his breath, thinking to himself about the absurdity of being breathless and near death from cold at the same time.

With his forearms, he pushed himself up once more and stumbled on towards Tony's. His legs had lost even more control from his brief respite, and he told himself not to take any more breaks.

As he rounded the last turn and saw the orange house, he exhaled violently to clear the shivers and stumbled up to the front gate. Once there, he leaned against it hard with his head and shoulders and closed his eyes. Taking a deep breath, he hit the door hard with his numb fists. No matter how hard he struck the wood, his hands felt nothing, as if they were just wooden clubs.

Less than a minute passed before Tony unlocked the latch and opened the door, Cole falling down to the wood entrance.

"Jesus, Cole. What the fuck?"

Cole coughed to clear some saltwater from his lungs and coiled himself in a ball, mouthing the words, "I need some help, Tony."

Tony was dragging him inside as he asked again, "What happened?"

"I got a bit wet."

As Tony slammed the door shut behind him, he smiled. "Ya think?"

Cole was powerless to help as Tony pulled at his shirt, boots, and pants to get the soaking clothes off of him. Once down to his boxers, Tony picked him up as best he could and dragged him to the bathtub. He then ran the water and turned once more to Cole, "What do you need?"

Cole, now free from his soaking clothing, felt the first hint of something warmer than the North Atlantic in the winter. He smiled. "A beer?"

"Dammit, Cole, come on. You're fucking purple."

Tony's concern brought Cole back to the reality of his situation. He was perhaps hypothermic, and it caused him to pause for a moment. Oddly enough, Cole thought back to Harley. Once more, he'd pushed himself to his limits and took a morbid pleasure in wandering an uncertain path between life and death.

Tony checked the water, then flipped Cole over the side as he fell into the tub. He couldn't feel the water at all. Scolding hot or ice cold, he had no idea. His neck was tense and he shuddered again in the tub.

"Are my toes still there?"

Tony looked at him for a moment, then shook his head. "Yeah."

"Seriously, Tony. Can you get me a beer?"

"You wouldn't be able to hold it if I did."

This was true, and Cole nodded. He felt the water against his back as it filled the tub. It was warm, and he thought that perhaps he'd be all right.

Tony looked at him sternly. "What did you do?"

Cole turned as best he could to face the side of the tub away from Tony. "I killed some people, Tony."

CHAPTER 14: ON THE ROCKS

COLE WOKE IN HIS bed, his fingers painful as he tried to make a fist and squeeze some life back into them. He was physically and mentally wiped, unsure of whether his body or mind had taken more of a beating the previous night. He didn't know how he'd gotten back to his bed, but as he blinked and cleared his thoughts, he faintly recalled Tony helping him out of the bath and into some warm clothes. By the light outside, he was certain it must be midday.

After laying there and staring at the ceiling for another 20 minutes, he finally rolled and sat up in his bed. As the blanket fell from around his shoulders, he shivered with a renewed chill. His arms instinctively curled up around him and he shuddered, remembering the hopelessness he'd fought back as he watched the imminent approach of the Atlantic Ocean. Pulling a sweatshirt over his head, he put some weight on his feet and tried to stand. Hundreds of pinpricks struck at the bottom of his feet and he sat back down, wincing in pain. He slowly rolled his ankles, wiggled his toes, and worked up the nerve to try once more.

He hobbled across his room, taking evenly spaced painful steps to the door. Pausing with his hand on the doorknob, he took a breath and made his way into the living room. As he worked his way towards the kitchen, Tony was bounding down the stairs and before reaching the main level, he said, "You've got like five minutes to tell me what happened."

"What?"

"Carl's on his way over. You'd better fill me in quick."

Cole leaned against the counter to take the weight off of his feet. He was almost out of breath from the pain. "Can you make some coffee?"

"Cole, I'm not fucking around right now. What happened?"

Cole pushed himself away from the counter, turning for the couch. "After midnight, I saw a boat with some dudes loading bags, same things we saw the other night. I'm pretty certain Carl was there, too."

"OK…and?"

Reaching the couch, Cole fell lazily to his side and pulled a blanket over himself. He rested his head against a cushion and exhaled. "Tony, seriously, can you make some coffee?"

Tony headed for the kitchen. "Sure, but keep talking."

"I was going to come get you, but they started casting off lines and got underway. So I hopped on the stern."

"Keep it coming, Cole."

"Two guys were linked up with the *North Star*. They admitted that much. And they were running to Ireland with guns and maybe cash."

"Maybe?"

"I didn't have enough time to go digging through everything."

"So how did the boat end up run up on the rocks near Cape Spear?"

Cole thought for a moment. "It ran aground?"

"Yup. Locals called it in at first light today—the *Kristen Ashley*."

Cole chewed at his lip, playing in his mind the wind and the current that may have carried it south. More likely, without anyone at the helm, the swells had simply pushed her to starboard, hard to the south, then drove her into the rocks.

Tony was brewing coffee, the first hint of it wafting across from the kitchen. Cole shivered once more and pulled the blanket up higher to his chest. He felt like shit.

Tony asked, "And the two guys? What happened to them?"

"They're the ones I killed."

"How?"

Cole grinned. "With a pistol."

He heard the spoon stirring in sugar and a moment later, Tony was bringing him a steaming mug. Taking a seat next to Cole, he leaned in, his expression one of curiosity more than anger.

"How did you get a gun?"

Cole smiled and took the mug into the palms of both his hands, feeling the warmth against his still semi-numb fingers. "You mean, how did I get a gun in Canada?"

"Yeah."

Taking his first sip, Cole held it in his mouth for a moment, then felt the warmth down his throat and into his gut. *Far worse things to be addicted to,* Cole thought.

"I've got friends, you know."

Tony stared at him. "Apparently. What kind of gun was it?"

"Black powder, revolver. Pretty sure it was a .44 caliber."

Tony sat expressionless, staring at him in disbelief. "You're joking…"

Cole shook his head. "Nope."

"Where's it now?"

"I tucked it up in some rocks by the channel."

"So you jumped in and swam back; that's how you got soaked?"

Cole nodded, saying nothing as his mind lingered on his own near death the previous evening. He shuddered once again and took a long sip, almost burning his mouth before he swallowed.

A pounding at the door interrupted whatever follow-up questions Tony might have had. They looked at each other, their expressions indicating that both knew who was standing outside.

Tony got up and walked over as the visitor beat on the door once more. When Tony opened it, Carl walked in, staring at him for a moment before he turned to look at Cole.

"Where were you last night, Cole?"

"Dancing. On George Street."

"Bullshit," he said as he stormed over to the living room and ripped the blanket away from Cole.

"Hey, take it easy, Carl."

Carl asked, "What happened to you? You look like shit," as he looked Cole up and down.

"Food poisoning, maybe. I dunno."

Tony tried to diffuse the situation, asking, "So what's up with this boat, Carl?"

Carl turned and scowled at him. "It ran aground with two dead guys, both shot multiple times."

Cole probed, knowing the answer. "Anything else suspicious?"

"We're still searching. The boat rolled at least once before settling on its side, so there's shit up and down the rocks. It's a bloody fucking mess right now."

"So what can we do for you?" Tony asked.

"Don't lie to me, Cole. Did you have anything to do with this?"

"No; sorry, Carl. I may be guilty of a few too many whiskey drinks last night, but that's about it."

"How about you, Tony? Were you up again last night with your fucking binoculars watching boats?"

Tony put out a slight smile, telling Carl with his relaxed demeanor that he was well guarded from Carl's hasty threats.

"No, I was asleep last night; sorry. You think there was someone else on the boat?"

"Two fishermen don't just shoot each other. They drink, they fight, and they pass the fuck out, but they don't kill each other or themselves."

Tony nodded. "Well, I'm sorry we can't be of much help. Seems like St. John's has an uptick lately in violence. That's a shame."

Carl stared at him. "It would seem."

Cole, sitting quietly until that moment, couldn't hold back. He cleared his throat and mustered some strength to sit up a bit more. "Down in the States, we call that vigilante justice."

Carl clenched his jaw, flared his nostrils, and a violent shade of red spread across his face. "What the fuck is that supposed to mean?"

"Nothing, Carl. I'm just saying we had a time when men took things into their own hands." His eyes narrowed and he stared hard at Carl before continuing. "Some folks look back fondly on that kind of thing."

"You listen to me, Cole. I'm the law in this town. Me. No one else. Not you, not Tony, not the fucking governor, *me*."

Carl turned for the door and said under his breath, "I have somewhere to be."

Tony walked with him to the door as Carl strode out without another word. Locking the door behind him, Tony turned to Cole, looking at him for a moment before shifting his gaze to the harbor below.

Cole asked, "He's a problem, isn't he?"

"Yup. He's gonna be an issue."

He worked his way to the UnderBelly as Olivia's shift was ending. After nearly 24 hours, he still couldn't shake the chill from his core. As he sipped a beer, she knew something was off with him, but avoided asking him directly.

Playfully, she asked, "Where have you been?"

"Catching up on some sleep."

Growing serious, she wasn't mad but her mood had changed. "Don't lie to me, Cole."

Setting his beer down, he knew she was right. "I don't want to lie to you."

She leaned in close to him and tilted her head in a sexy yet commanding kind of way, replying, "Then don't."

"Can we go back to your place?"

She smiled at him, "Is this some kind of ploy to get me in bed?"

Cole cleared his throat, not taking his eyes off of hers. "I hadn't thought about that, but if it works, then maybe."

She went to wiping down the now-empty bartop. "You seem off. What's up with you?"

"Just a little cold."

She stopped wiping and asked, "Why?"

"I went swimming last night."

She left the cloth on the bar and walked over to him, checking the doorway into the kitchen to make sure they were alone.

"The fishing boat that sank?"

Cole turned away from her, looking towards the dark stone wall. "It didn't sink. It ran aground."

She put her hand up to cover her mouth when she pieced the rest together. As she spoke, the words took her breath with them. "With that gun?" She waited. "...Cole?"

He looked at her, unsure of what would transpire in the next few moments. The rest of whatever relationship they might have hung in uncertainty as she looked at him with confused eyes. The decision was hers to make.

"They were smuggling drugs."

She asked, almost in a begging tone, "Are you sure?"

"One hundred percent. Guns, too, going to Ireland."

She leaned to her side against the counter, and looked away towards the empty bar. Cole wanted nothing more than to climb over the counter to her and lock his arms around her slender waist. He knew, though, that she needed the space to make up her own mind. He hated the silence, but sat through it nonetheless. She walked to the far end, slipped around the corner, then walked back towards him. As she turned the corner, he had no idea what she'd do. He was relieved when she took a seat next to him. She kept a bit of distance between them and suddenly he sensed the conversation would not be a good one.

Taking a breath, Olivia spun towards him, her knee pressing against him. He had chills as soon as she touched him. "Are you all right?"

He was relieved and answered plainly, "I just can't get warm. It's been almost a full day."

She touched the palm of her hand against his cheek and scratched his stubble with the soft pads of her fingertips. He shuddered with chills again.

"Not sure if that's from the cold, or from you."

She smiled, her lips wearing a neutral shade of red, and he raised his hand to cup hers still against his cheek.

"You're hand is freezing."

"Yeah, I know."

Rubbing her knee against the side of his leg, she exhaled slowly, looking down and away again. The pause that followed told Cole she was still back and forth in her mind about him.

"You could have died."

"I came close."

Shivering once more, he shook the chill violently from him, mad at its persistent deep grip, saying, "Sorry. I can't stop."

She pulled her hand away from his cheek and stood up, taking his hand as she did.

"Come on. Let's get you out of here."

The morning light snuck in from between the wall and curtains, just enough for Cole to see her hand and the dark polish on her fingernails on his chest. His toes were cold, but he felt the warmth from Olivia as she slept pressed against his side. Bringing his hand up to rest on top of hers, he shifted his head against the pillow and closed his eyes.

He woke again when she stirred nearly an hour later. Rather than getting up, she pulled herself closer and draped one long leg over both of his. He was in much better spirits and turned to face her, pressing his face into the delicate skin of her neck.

"Feeling better?"

"Yeah, I am. Thanks."

He took a long deep breath and yawned, nudging himself closer against her neck. "I don't remember last night. What happened?"

"What do you mean?"

"Last night, once we got here."

She laughed out loud, pulling her head back to look at him. From the pillow, he looked up at her. "What?"

"You passed out before I even got into bed."

Disappointed in himself, he shrugged. "Hmmm."

She reached for his hand and played with each of his fingertips, rubbing them in between her thumb and index finger.

"At least you're not an ice cube anymore." Pausing for a brief second, she asked, "Was that the end of it?"

Cole shook his head. "No, I don't think so."

"What's next?"

"How much do you want to know?" he asked.

"Will it end?"

"One way or another."

She looked at his mouth, as if she was mad at the words, then looked back up into his eyes. "I don't like it when you talk like that."

He reached up and brushed her hair back. "Sorry."

With the passing minutes, Cole was certain he'd turned the page and was gaining his strength back. He rolled over, nearly on top of her, and kissed her lips. He shifted his hips, dug one knee under her far leg, and pulled himself closer once more.

She smiled, asking, "Everything working down there?"

He chewed at his lip. "Anywhere you gotta be today?"

She shook her head.

"Let's find out then."

CHAPTER 15: COMING TO BLOWS

THE PALEST OF blue light slipped into her room from the windows. A light crust of frost stuck to the glass outside, obscuring any more detail than the morning's first color. He'd been awake for some time, Olivia curled up and asleep next to him. Gently pulling his arm out from underneath her, he turned to his side and sat up, dropping his bare feet to the floor. The wood was cold, and he took a side step onto a rug that pressed against the wall. Stepping further, he pulled the curtain back and took a long look outside at the first hint of day to touch the two inches of fresh snow.

Downstairs, Cole took his time with a French press, boiling water on the stovetop before carefully pouring it over a heaping pile of coarse-ground coffee. He then sat at the kitchen in silence, wondering why he found himself thinking back to Marie and the games they used to play. He seemed to think of her most when his life was at a decision point, and he took that as a sign. His mood soured, and he let the coffee run longer as he sat and stared at the far wall in near total darkness.

As he poured his first cup, Olivia was moving around upstairs, the old boards creaking underneath her delicate footsteps. He smiled and cast aside the darker thoughts. Pouring a second cup for her, he stirred in a spoonful of sugar with cream and set it down next to his. A minute later, she was seated by his side and took her first small sip. Cole stood up, just behind her right shoulder, and wrapped his arm around her chest then over her left shoulder. He pulled himself in close, pressing his lips into the side of her neck, taking a deep breath and kissing at her skin.

"What's that for?"

"No reason at all," he said as he sat back down to look at her.

She smiled, almost blushing, as if that was something that she might ever do, then dipped her head to take another careful sip. Her hair fell in front of her face and a few random shallow curls accentuated the lighter shades of brown in her hair.

"Are you feeling any better?"

Cole thought for a moment, half-expecting to break out in a shiver again. As the seconds passed, he felt his strength had now come back.

"Yeah. I think last night did the trick."

She laughed and looked away, pretending to focus on her cup. "What are you doing today?"

Cole took a long sip and thought about what to tell her. He didn't want to lie, so he settled for a partial truth. "I need to do some laundry at some point. Might go into town, too, and try to find someone."

She asked, "Who?"

"A detective."

She said nothing, but looked at him with curious eyes, asking in her own way to continue with his thoughts.

"I've got some information for him."

It's the truth, he thought.

"Which one?" she asked.

Her tone caught him off guard, and he answered before his thoughts caught up with him. "Carl. You know him?"

She stiffened in her seat. "The Irish one?"

"I think he's from here."

She replied coldly. "His family is from Ireland."

Concerned, Cole asked, "So you know him?"

Looking away, Olivia nodded. "He's a piece of shit."

"Why do you say that?"

"No reason. I don't want to talk about it."

Changing the subject, she got up and walked around to the small kitchen, her hips hidden only by a short pair of gym shorts and an over-sized sweatshirt hanging from her shoulders.

Regaining her senses, she asked, "Breakfast?"

"Nah. I should get going." He said it knowing that he'd waste the day away with her if given the chance. "But thanks."

An hour later, he was wandering the narrow gravel trail along a cliff to find the spot where he'd climbed up two nights prior. The dark wet rocks at the bottom were indistinguishable from each other. Small waves of clear water rolled gently over them, the sound of their breaking against the cliff echoing upwards and ricocheting in an unending calming chorus. He felt the breeze against his face and paused to look out towards the open Atlantic. The same persistent fog bank hung low on the horizon, but had not yet reached the shore of Newfoundland.

Looking down, Cole cursed under his breath as he looked for the small sliver of loose rock that he'd scaled in the frigid night. Digging his hands deep in his pockets and sniffling hard to keep his nose from running with the cold breeze, he walked on another 15 yards. Up at the edge, he looked down again at the seaweed, all of it shimmering like a pile of worn pennies from under a foot of saltwater. Something about the formation caught his attention, and he looked to his right at the concrete ledge where the small navigation beacon was mounted.

The spacing seemed right, so he carefully stepped off the trail, avoiding a near-vertical 20-foot tall crevice with smaller rocks between two large slabs of dark stone. At the bottom, he was standing precariously at the edge, the waves lapping against the grey stone not more than a foot below him. The ocean was far louder than it had been at the trail above him. He could smell the rawness of the salt air as he crouched down and looked for the rock where he'd stashed his jacket and gun.

Voices above caused him to press his body against the sheer cliff until they trailed off towards the east. Scavenging again, he found the tail end of his jacket behind and inconspicuous circular stone. It was still damp as he brushed away a layer of ice and tucked it under his arm.

Navigating back to the crevice, he tried with one arm to find a good hold, but couldn't. Standing for a minute more, he looked for a better path but found none.

Fuck, he thought as he set the holster and pistol down and shook out the damp jacket. He set it down and picked up the damp leather holster. It was soft to the touch and freezing cold as he slung it crossways over his shoulder. Then he pulled on his jacket and pressed his arms through the sleeves, wearing the cold gear to make his climb easier. He was enveloped in a blanket of cold and hurried up the rock face to the trail above. Drops of icy water ran down the length of his sleeves and stung at his fingers before they fell to the gravel at his feet.

Reaching the top, he took off the jacket and gun and balled them up under one arm. His sweatshirt was now blotted with wet spots, and he clenched his fists to stem the cold as he tucked the bundle under his arm and hurried back to Tony's house. Reaching the front door, he unlocked it and slipped inside, hoping that Tony wouldn't emerge from upstairs like he often did. Thankfully he wasn't home, and Cole tossed his jacket in the washing machine then proceeded to the kitchen to take the gun apart and clean it.

With one pin removed, the barrel slid off easily enough, followed by the cylinder. He dropped them both into the faucet and put the water on hot, adding dish detergent to the mix. With some random utensils from the drawer and a sacrificial dish towel torn into thin strips, he was able to work the suds from the sink into the corners and crevices of the hammer channel. The black powder had left a thick layer of gunk that clung to the brass frame, requiring more elbow grease than Cole anticipated to wipe away.

The barrel and cylinder were both dirty and required several iterations of scrubbing and soaking to clean. Half an hour passed and Cole's fingers were painful from the work, but the parts were clean enough to reassemble. He took one last look down the barrel, holding it up towards the light over the kitchen to confirm that he'd removed the bulk of the residue. He dried it with a second dishtowel, looking at the black stains on it with disdain after he'd dried it. It was still dirty. Far from inspection ready, but, if given a good time to dry out, the piece would work just fine. Cole was certain he may need it again.

He disassembled it again, setting all the parts aside in his room to give them ample time to dry, then went back to the kitchen and cooked himself his first meal of the day. Tony walked in as Cole sat devouring a plate of eggs and salsa, having disposed of the dirty towels in the trash outside.

Setting his jacket down, Tony asked, "Where you been?"

"With Olivia."

"All morning?"

"Yup."

Tony walked into the kitchen, pausing for a moment at the sink, before he took a seat at the table with Cole.

"And this afternoon?"

Cole smiled, with a mouthful of eggs, not caring to hide the devilish look on his face. He chewed some more, swallowed, and took another long sip of coffee.

"Might go have a chat with Carl."

Tony said nothing, licking at his chapped lower lip and looking down.

With concern, he asked, "You got a plan?"

Cole nodded, "Yup."

"Careful, Cole."

He lurked up and down George Street, finally resigning himself to a familiar wooden stool at Green Sleeves. It was nearing 11 at night, and Ryan was at it again with his guitar up on stage. To his left a pretty redhead playing fiddle held the entire bar captive with her rhythm. She lazily pulled at the strings while her tempo wandered somewhere from just behind to in lock step with Ryan. It was, in all likelihood, her style of playing, and Cole was consumed by it. In turn, Ryan seemed to feed off of her energy and put that much more into the notes he sang and played. The dance floor was nearing a riot, and despite Cole's motives for the evening, he drained the last of his pint and slid a bill towards the bartender. Carl would have to wait.

Up on his feet, he trolled for no more than half the length of the floor before a dangerously dark-haired woman of St. John's locked eyes with him. She offered no resistance when he casually let out his left hand, fingers extending towards her. A moment passed and he slowly spun her twice to the pace of the fiddle then pulled her in close. She tried to hide her surprise as he picked up the pace and they joined in the revelry of another George Street evening. Two songs later he took her friend and did the same. It was some time later, Cole now in dangerous territory, when he glanced at his watch and noted it was nearly midnight. Like hungry wolves, the two women waited and whispered among themselves as he sipped at another beer to compose his thoughts. The first one approached and made light conversation, clearly testing the waters and looking for more.

It was time for him to escape. As midnight came and went, Cole excused himself, grinning at his good fortune of making it out of the bar unscathed. Out in the street, he felt the wind hit small beads of sweat along the top of his forehead. Taking long breaths of the frozen and still air, he zipped up his jacket and dug his hands deep into his pockets. He leaned against the wall and waited.

Twenty minutes passed before he heard a commotion from the entrance to one of the seedier clubs next door. He'd never bothered to check the name, but knew that the younger rowdy crowd tended to congregate there. Looking up through the second-floor windows, it appeared the dance floor was full of St. John's youth all having violent seizures to some god-awful techno-trance music. A bouncer wearing a tight black shirt was struggling to partially lift and carry out a drunk kid. Cole watched for a minute to see if any his friends emerged in his defense. Satisfied a minute later that the kid was alone as he argued loudly from the street in drunken gibberish, Cole approached and bumped into him forcefully with his shoulder then continued walking.

The kid yelled, "Hey, motherfucker…"

Cole turned, his hands still deep in his pockets, and said nothing. He was walking slowly backwards, his eyes locked on the kid. He shrugged his shoulders and smiled mockingly. It worked.

The kid stumbled towards him. "Fuck you…"

Cole laughed again, realizing that the poor kid couldn't even put words together. "You want to fuck me?" Cole stopped stepping backwards and stood in the inch of crusted brown ice in the street.

The kid stumbled. "I didn't say that." He inched closer towards him.

Cole egged him on. "Well, fuck you too."

The kid lunged at him, and Cole slammed his open palm into the side of his head and deflected him towards the curb. He spun wildly around, nearly falling down before regaining his footing and squaring up again with Cole. As he took a step forward with his left foot and closed with both feet, Cole threw a right cross and caught the kid squarely in the jaw, knocking him out cold. *That was too easy*, he thought as he stood and exhaled forcefully to slow his mildly elevated heart rate.

He stood there for nearly two minutes as the kid regained his balance and sat up, looking blankly at Cole. As his mind caught up to him, the kid tried to stand up. Cole pressed his boot into his chest and sat him back down, saying calmly, "Just stay there, bud."

The kid pushed Cole's foot aside and used both his hands to steady himself. As he stood up and was about to make eye contact with Cole once more, he was knocked back by another downward cross from Cole and slumped once more to the icy street. Looking around, Cole could see that a small crowd had gathered. He scanned the audience briefly looking for any of the kid's friends, but if there were any among the onlookers, none stepped forward to challenge Cole.

Come on, he thought. Another minute passed before he heard the sirens. As the first police car slowly edged its way through the crowd, Cole kicked lightly at the kid, who was now on his hands and knees, to knock him down once more. A police officer waded through the crowd, clearly not in a hurry, and approached Cole.

"What happened?"

"This guy's drunk. He attacked me."

As he spoke, the kid was clambering up to his knees once more, the left side of his face already swollen and red. Perhaps still dazed from two solid punches, he fell back down to his ass and stared up and towards the flashing red lights of an ambulance pulling up.

Cole spoke calmly, "I'd like to file a report."

The officer took a breath, and looked away towards his partner who was sitting on the hood of their patrol car. He motioned him over with a subtle nod. "He wants to file a report."

Confused, the second officer asked, "Why?"

Cole fought to contain a grin. "He attacked me."

"Come on, bud, no harm done here. Just a little scrap. We'll take him and get him patched up."

"Sorry to be a pain, but I really need to file a report. I'd actually like to speak with Carl."

Both officers looked at each, unsure of who Cole was referring to.

"The detective, Carl."

They looked dismissively at each other.

"If I need to go hit him again, I will. Or I'll find another one to knock out until I can talk to Carl."

One officer shifted his weight, as if to intervene. Cole defused the situation, asking again, "Can you please call Carl? I really need to speak with him."

"How do you know him?"

Cole grinned. "We're old drinking buddies."

One of the officers laughed out loud while the other looked at him imploring him to hide his amusement. The first guy cleared his throat, pulled out his phone and stepped away while the other stayed with Cole.

He heard the first one on the phone raise his voice, "I don't know, Sir. He says he knows you."

Carl was likely yelling at him as he spoke again into the phone. "Sir, he knocked this kid out, and now he said he needs to speak with you. He wants to file a report."

Hanging up and putting his phone away, he returned to Cole and the other officer, kicking at a large piece of ice on the street.

"Well, he isn't happy."

Cole asked, "Is he coming?"

"Yeah. Give him a few minutes."

Both officers looked at each other with some unspoken level of uncertainty. Cole thought perhaps he should probe deeper, but opted to keep his secrets to himself. Both officers tended to the drunk as one of the paramedics tried to help him to the back of the waiting ambulance. Too drunk for his own good, the kid mouthed off and was soon in handcuffs being walked off instead to the waiting cruiser.

Behind the patrol car, Cole saw a solitary flashing blue light in the grill of an unmarked car. Cole walked towards it, unable to make out the driver through the blinding headlights pointed directly at him. He walked to the passenger side and leaned over as the window slowly lowered. Carl stared at him with a pissed look on his face.

"What the fuck are you doing here?"

"Looking for love, Carl." He paused, smiled and continued. "We need to talk."

Carl looked ahead at the crowd. The bars of George Street were on the verge of spilling their patrons out for the final hour of debauchery. "Not here. Get in."

Cole reluctantly got in, thinking through his options as Carl backed the car away and turned down a street leading away from George Street.

Impatiently, he asked, "What?"

"I killed your guys."

Carl continued driving, but turned and stared at Cole, showing no emotion. He gripped the steering wheel with both hands and turned down an alley, speeding along for 20 yards before screeching to a halt. Cole readied himself, and as he did, Carl pulled his gun from his holster and aimed it at Cole's head. Cole blocked it with his left hand and slammed Carl's hand against the headrest. He then felt the weight of Carl's left fist striking his upper cheek. As Carl reared back to strike again, Cole answered with his own fist to Carl's lower lip, busting it open. As he recoiled, Carl landed a punch just over Cole's right eye. They punched at each other for a few more seconds, neither landing decisive hits. Cole abandoned the tactic and grabbed Carl by the neck and Carl did the same, leaving both of them partially choked and unable to move in the cramped car.

Groaning, Cole said, "You got another boat?"

Still choking, Carl replied, his own voice strained, "You're fucking dead."

"I'll drive your boat."

Relaxing his grip on Cole' neck, Carl cleared his throat as Cole returned the favor. They sat there in a stalemate, both staring at each other. Carl's nostrils flared as rage boiled in his eyes. "I ought to kill you, you little fuck."

"I want a cut, Carl." Thinking back to the sage words of long-dead smugglers who'd crossed paths with Cole, he smirked. "It's just business, Carl."

CHAPTER 16: UNCHARTED WATERS

TONY SAT EXPRESSIONLESS in a chair, looking out the big window as the dozen or so shades of greyscale seemed to cut sharp horizontal lines across the sky. He hadn't moved in five minutes, leaving Cole increasingly uncomfortable. It was the middle of the afternoon, and he'd be meeting Carl downtown by the inner wharf after sunset to check out a boat. Sitting on the couch, Cole thought back to the night prior and the shimmer of Carl's gun as he'd effortlessly drawn it on Cole. Drunk or not, Carl was a gunfighter. He smiled a bit at the recollection of his reaction, knowing that Harley would've approved of the speed with which Cole had brushed it aside.

In his left hand, he held a semi-thawed bag of corn. His right temple was swollen, but he'd iced it as much as his skin would allow, and the cold permeated deep into his head. Carl had not escaped unharmed, as Cole was certain he too was holed up somewhere and icing his own wounds.

"I don't know, Cole."

Cole looked over at him, ruffling the clumps of frozen corn in the bag and pressing it once more to his head.

"Don't know about what?"

"Whoever these guys are, they might just kill you."

Cole looked at him with his one good eye. "Or I'll kill them."

After another pause, Tony exhaled long and slow.

Cole asked, "Can we get some backup?"

"For this, not a chance. I'm way outside of my swim lane on this one."

Cole nodded, setting the bag of corn back down in his lap.

"What time you meeting him?" Tony asked.

"Around six."

"You going alone?"

Cole smiled, knowing the answer before he asked, "Do you want to tag along?"

Tony nodded, stood up slowly, and walked upstairs. As he passed Cole, he patted his shoulder. "I'm gonna crash for a bit."

By five that evening, a menacing sky was already shedding the last bits of grey as the darkness rolled in and over St. John's. In his room, Cole was tinkering with the revolver. Some of the water had left small rust marks, and he chipped away at them with a small bit of steel wool he'd grabbed from the kitchen. Working some oil into it, the rust lifted and left blemishes where the blueing had been worn off. He oiled the cylinder and barrel, wiping a thick coat inside and out with a rag and then wiping more still with another to leave a thin film over the entire pistol. He was now quite fond of the piece, feeling some kind of bond with the old gun and its rough wooden grips.

He poured some powder into each chamber, plugged it with a greased wool patch, then set a soft lead ball on the mouth of it, rotating and pushing with the rod to fully seat the bullet. With his finger, he plucked out the thin ring of lead that had been sliced away by the seating of each round. With six chambers loaded, he rested the hammer down on a detent in between two of them and took one last admiring look at the revolver. He felt the length of the barrel with the palm of his left hand. The steel was cold to the touch, as if the gun had not quite recovered from its swim several days prior.

Cole tucked it into the holster and slung it crossways over his shoulder. His jacket was still wet in some places as he pulled it on, zipping it partially before stepping out into the living room. Tony was at the dining room table where they never did much of anything. On it sat three Pelican cases, and Cole could see, even from across the room, that

Tony was loading magazines with pistol ammo. He walked closer in partial disbelief.

"What the fuck is this?"

Tony kept pressing .45 ACP rounds into a black Glock magazine. Not looking away from the task at hand, he spoke matter-of-factly, "You didn't think I had some supplies?"

"Nope. Where's this stuff been?"

Tony topped off a magazine, set it down, and went to work loading a second. "Under the couch."

Cole laughed and unzipped his jacket, pulling out the pistol and setting it down gently on the table.

The magazine clicked again as Tony pressed in a round before stopping and looking at Cole's revolver. He swallowed, a smirk on his face, and stared at it in partial disbelief.

"Serious?"

Cole rolled up on the balls of his feet, then back down to heels, declaring with pride, "Yup."

Tony reached for it, picking the revolver up in the palm of his hand.

Cole said, "Careful—she's loaded."

"Jesus, Cole. Did you test it before the other night?"

"Nope. But it works."

Tony set it back down and looked at Cole. "Apparently."

He picked up a magazine and a single round of .45, asking, "You want one of these?"

Cole smiled. "Nah. I'm kind of partial to this thing now." He picked up the revolver and tucked it back in the holster under his armpit.

Finishing with the third magazine, Tony loaded one into the full-frame Glock, then tucked it into a holster at the small of his back. The remaining two magazines went into his pockets. Further down the table, Tony picked up a short-barreled M4, locked the bolt back, and smashed a 30-round magazine into it before dropping the bolt and chambering a round. Cole smiled at the familiar ping that echoed around the living room.

"I'll hang back in the shadows, but I'll be watching."

Cole nodded. "Thanks."

Once outside, Tony drove down from the Battery and parked along the easternmost edge of the wharf. With the small truck shut down, Cole found the silence uncomfortable, and he reached quickly to open the door.

"Cole…"

Cole stopped, his hand resting on the latch. "Yeah?"

"Careful, OK?"

"You got it." He unlocked the door, stepped outside into the cold and damp air, and zipped up his jacket, pulling the hood snug against his head. As he walked west towards the crowded inner docks, he felt the wind behind him, pressing against his jacket but not penetrating yet. *Fair winds*, he thought. Not looking back, he knew that Tony would soon be on the move as well, hustling from one dark corner to another. Although Cole knew it was an illusion, with Tony behind him, he felt some sort of invincibility.

Beyond the main wharf sat several dry docks, with a smaller wharf around it littered with boats, many of which were in permanent disrepair. It was a graveyard for most, the long-abandoned hopes and dreams of Newfoundland fishermen who'd fallen on hard times. The active fleet was tied up just east along the downtown wharf, but here sat the sad few, many listing to one side and near the point where they'd be plucked from the water one final time and sold for scrap. He wandered the perimeter of the docks until his eyes centered on Carl standing by a nondescript concrete building with another man.

He approached with caution, trying to convey the same confidence with which he'd started the walk. Stopping a few feet from Carl, he nodded and sniffled to stop his nose from running. A light mist fell from above, barely enough to wet his jacket, and he was still warm from the walk. Carl stared hard at him, and Cole wondered if he wasn't toying with the idea of killing him right there.

"Cole, this is Matt."

Cole nodded at the guy, who only now looked towards the two of them and nodded back.

"Matt owes me a favor."

Cole wasn't sure what that meant, and looked back and forth at the two of them.

Carl continued, his eyes growing wider, "He's lending me his boat for a week."

Cole now understood. "Great. Where is she?"

Turning around, the man pointed at a white superstructure and red hull that was tied up behind them. Cole could see it was a fresh coat of paint with the words *Mary Emmalene* painted just under the forward rail. With any boat, looks were often deceiving, but she immediately caught his eye. Matt turned and took a step towards his boat with Cole taking a half step to follow. He caught some quick movement by Carl and turned to see the pistol pointed at him. There was three or four feet of distance between them, too much for Cole to swipe the gun like he had in Carl's car.

Carl, his eyes fixed on Cole, spoke softly, "Matt, take a walk."

Cole took a breath and watched as Matt walked towards his boat in no particular hurry. Distracted from his predicament, Cole was impressed with Matt's seemingly casual approach to Cole's impending execution. He looked back at Carl, thinking perhaps Carl might smile. Instead, he was still flaring his nostrils and even in the darkness, his cheeks growing red. Cole extended both of his hands outwards, declaring, "You got me."

Carl's arm was shaking, and it occurred to Cole that he was genuinely pissed off and ready to kill him. A small dot of red light then zigzagged for a moment across Carl's chest before steadying dead center on his chest. Cole let out a half chuckle. Carl responded by locking down his jaw, the muscles in his cheeks now tense. Cole was now following the laser as it wobbled back and forth an inch from side to side. From the shadows, Tony was locked on.

Carl stabbed forward with his pistol and grumbled, "What the fuck are you grinning at?"

The laser drifted upwards, to his neck, chin, and finally to his eyes where Tony wiggled it laterally just a bit to get his attention. Carl flinched, closing both his eyes and tried to swat the laser away to no avail. Cole took a side step to clear himself from the gun, then lunged forward, taking out Carl at the knees. He folded and collapsed hard to the concrete, and Cole used the momentum to work his way up to Carl's torso, where he doubled up his grip on Carl's right hand, isolating the pistol. Carl fought for a moment, but he was no match to Cole's solid mounted position. Cole wrestled for the gun and after a few moments of Carl's stubbornness, he dropped three consecutive left elbows onto Carl's face, opening up a just-closed wound from their tussle in the car. Blood poured out from it, enough that Carl eased his grip, and Cole had the pistol in his hands a moment later. With both of his knees now pressed into the meat of Carl's biceps, he was powerless to even defend himself. Cole was not upset, but he thought for a moment of how Carl had most certainly intended to kill him. He dropped the magazine from Carl's gun, racked the slide to clear the loaded round, and pistol-whipped Carl hard across his cheek, opening up another gash in his face. Carl spit blood at him, and Cole reared back to strike him again, stopping only when he heard Tony's voice.

"Cole…"

He held the pistol by its slide, his left arm across his body with his clenched fist behind him, ready to deliver a sweeping blow of the grip to bust Carl open some more.

Tony spoke again, calmly saying, "Cole…"

He let his arm down gently, with Carl wiggling and uselessly trying to free himself.

"Yup. I know."

He locked eyes with Carl, who still had an internal fire raging. With the upper hand, he was in control, but it reaffirmed what Cole had suspected for some time. Carl would kill him. Or Cole would kill Carl. Those were the only options.

The two of them rolled Carl to his side, and Tony produced a roll of tape with which they locked his wrists together behind his back. He groaned as they taped him up, and Carl tried as best he could to wrestle himself free. They stood him up and Carl shook himself again. Tony held on firm to one arm but Cole let go, rearing back and striking the side of Carl's face with a hard cross, the knuckles of his pointer and middle finger hitting cleanly against the outline of his jaw. He fell towards Tony, who fought for a moment to keep Carl upright.

"Cole, quit it."

"My bad."

Tony moved forward with him, carrying much of Carl's weight as he stumbled to regain his footing. Cole looked towards the boat to see that Matt was standing casually on the deck, leaning against the wheelhouse, his arms crossed in front of him. Matt was not phased by any of it. They both walked Carl to the edge of the wharf and Tony asked, "You got him?"

"Yup," Cole replied.

Tony hopped across the low rail and down to the deck before turning to help Carl over. As he turned, Cole pushed Carl from behind and let go of his arm, smiling as Carl tumbled forward, landing hard on the wooden deck.

"Oops," he said with deliberate insincerity.

"Dammit, Cole."

Defensively, and still standing on the wharf, Cole pointed down at the now barely conscious Carl. "You know he keeps trying to kill me, right?"

Frustrated, Tony turned to Matt, who still hadn't budged from his position against the wheelhouse. "Would you excuse us for a bit?" Tony asked.

Matt shrugged, not saying a word about Carl's bloodied body on the deck of his boat, and stepped back up onto the wharf, walking east as if out for a nightly stroll. Tony and Cole watched him disappear and Tony turned to ask, "Can you help me get him inside?"

Cole hopped down. "Sure."

Once inside, they leaned Carl against a bulkhead, and the two of them sat opposite of him on a greasy and worn-down cushioned bench seat. Carl's head rolled as he fought to regain his composure. A minute passed before Tony spoke.

"Where are the guns going, Carl?"

"Fuck you, asshole."

Cole stood up and took a step towards Carl, who tucked his head instinctively into his shoulder and closed his eyes.

"Cole, sit."

He did as Tony had asked, crossing his legs out in front of himself and rolling his boots under the light of an exposed bulb. The toe of his right boot was shiny and damp. He pressed his leg farther forward and wiped it on the leg of Carl's jeans. Sure enough, it was blood, and Cole grinned, looking directly at Carl as he did. Carl exhaled loudly and slumped a bit further.

"Where are the guns going?"

"You're a bunch of fucking hypocrites."

Calmly, Tony asked, "Why is that?"

"Where do you think they're coming from? The guns..." He paused and looked up at the two of them, before continuing. "They're coming from the States, you self-righteous twats. You assholes have your second amendment and your fucking guns. Why shouldn't the rest of the world have them, too?"

"You mean the New Irish Republican Army?"

Cole eyes grew wide as he looked at Tony. He'd always known he was smart, but perhaps he'd underestimated Tony's cleverness.

Carl angrily replied, "You're fucking right I do. What does it matter to you, Tony?" He spit more blood on the floor and breathed heavily through his nostrils, "We don't want anything more than what you've done. You went to war, why can't we? How's that any fucking different?"

Cole's mind was racing, connecting the various dots of the past few months. Tony was far ahead of him, asking quickly, "And the drugs?"

Carl rolled his head. "What about the fucking drugs?"

"That was your idea, too?"

"And now you're some goddamned moral authority?"

Tony shifted his legs and mulled it over. "I'm not saying that, but killing your own people?"

Carl snorted back, "Those aren't my people. I did St. John's a favor."

"Lot of dead people here in St. John's, even if they're not 'your' people." Tony fired back.

Carl stared out the open hatch to the deck, then slowly turned back to Cole and Tony. "Some asshole mixes a tablespoon instead of a teaspoon and a bunch of addicts off themselves? You'd have me feel bad for that?"

Tony pressed on. "Who buys the drugs, you or someone else?"

Carl turned and looked forward to the helm, refusing to answer. Cole turned slightly to see Tony motion him on with his head. Cole hopped up, grabbed Carl's mangled bloody hair, and pressed his head against the wood paneling. With his left leg, he reared back and drove his knee hard into the left side of Carl's torso. Tony sat motionless as Carl moaned.

They paused, Cole still holding a fistful of Carl's hair, his head still pressed against the wood.

"Where's this boat going, Carl? Drugs or guns?"

Carl said nothing. Cole turned to look for a cue to strike again, but Tony calmly raised one finger from his right hand that rested easily on his lap.

"Let me guess, Carl. You need to sell some more drugs on George Street to buy some more guns to make up for the ones that didn't make it."

Carl stared up at him, defeat showing on his battered face. Cole wrestled Carl's head back and forth a few more times before letting go. He turned to Tony, who said nothing for a moment. He was thinking, and Cole knew to wait patiently. Then Tony looked at him, wiped at his cheek with his left hand, and shrugged his shoulders. "Well, I think that's enough for now."

COLE AND TONY STOOD on the wharf, leaving Carl tied up down in the wheelhouse. The mist had grown thick, but still hadn't turned into the heavy rain that was hung up in the darkness above. Cole could almost feel the clouds wrestling among themselves over his head and knew it was only a matter of time.

"It'll be morning soon. I should call the governor."

Cole tried to hide his disapproval. "You gonna turn him in?"

Tony nodded. "This is a mess. Way over our heads at this point."

"So who takes it from here?"

Tony breathed deeply, exhaling with some of his own dissatisfaction. "I dunno. Maybe the State Department can throw some resources. Fuck, maybe the UN." He paused. "Assuming they want to do anything with it."

Cole pivoted slowly to watch Tony's eyes. "And Ireland?"

He was caught off-guard by the question. "What about Ireland?"

"The guns, and the drugs. Carl's linked up with some bad folks over there."

Tony cleared his throat and pulled his collar up close around his neck. Beads of water had formed on his head and were beginning to run down his neck. "That's the other side of the Atlantic, Cole. Not for us to pick that fight."

Neither of them spoke as a minute passed.

"What about Carl?"

Tony laughed under his breath. "Not really anywhere for him to go in the shape he's in. We can hand him off to the governor in the morning."

"You want me to keep an eye on him until then?"

Tony looked at him suspiciously.

"I'll keep him here," said Cole. "You can send the cops down to the boat first thing in the morning."

Not letting go of his doubts, Tony shook his head. "Not so sure you won't kill him."

"Come on, Tony. A few hours and I'll meet you back at the house after they pick him up."

Tony looked out towards the dark harbor and the Battery beyond. "You're up to something."

Cole looked away, hoping Tony wouldn't see too far into his plan.

Tony exhaled. "Fine," he said, leaving Cole uncertain of his true feelings on the matter.

Several hours had passed and Cole was soaked, sitting on a low rock wall the formed the perimeter of the parking lot atop Signal Hill. A faint and distant trace of orange streaked across the eastern horizon and gave some better perspective to the thick menacing clouds above. They were the kind that seemed interwoven, tangled up like a pit of snakes that slithered in random directions across the sky. A light but persistent rain fell, and Cole had taken his time to let the water soak through all of his clothes.

He looked back at Carl's car, the windows fogged up from his bloodied beat-up body in the backseat. Standing up, Cole walked over and opened the passenger door. Carl had nodded off, and Cole nudged his shoulder with his boot to wake him up. Opening his eyes, Carl recoiled and stared hard at Cole, exhaling loudly to catch his breath.

"Get out."

"Fuck off."

Reaching inside, Cole grabbed his damp jacket and pulled him out sideways until Carl fell to the pavement. He took both Carl's sleeves just above the elbows and slowly dragged him up to his feet. Leaning against the side of the car, Carl took a look to the east, as fingers of dark grey worked their way among the low clouds and the increasing rain blotted out the line of orange on the distant horizon.

"What do you want?"

Cole took out a knife and cut away the tape holding Carl's hands behind his back.

"I want to drive that boat."

With force, Carl snarled, "Go fuck yourself, you little shit."

"You don't give me enough credit, Carl. How much can you offer?"

Carl stared at him, flaring his nostrils like he always did.

"What about Tony?"

Cole grinned for a half second. "I'll deal with Tony. How soon can you have that boat ready?"

Carl was silent, mulling it over in his head before replying, "Two days. Two percent of the cut, should work to a thousand, Canadian."

"Four percent, and I'll get your boat there and back."

Carl looked away and spit some more of his blood to the pavement, "And Tony?"

"I'll talk to him this morning, tell him to wait a few more days before he calls anyone, and that I'm gonna sink it."

Carl coughed and spit again, wiping at his lip with a trembling hand. "And what makes you think he'll wait?"

"He doesn't want anything to do with any of this. If this whole thing just up and disappeared tomorrow, he'd be a much happier guy. So why don't you make the call?"

"Call?"

Cole shrugged. "Yeah. Call your guy, you tell them I'm leaving in two days, and we'll be all settled. Four percent."

Carl snarled back, "Three."

Cole grinned. "Fine."

With reluctance, Carl pulled out his phone and dialed, holding it up to his right ear. He took a breath and said, "I can have another boat in two days."

Carl listened and nodded, looking at Cole as he did. When it was his turn to speak again, he nodded once more and said, "Fifty thousand. Once that starts moving, I'll let you know about the next run."

Carl nodded some more, looking displeased as he did, saying, "I know, I've got a new guy. His name is Cole."

Carl nodded twice more, rubbing under his nose with his left fingers, then looking at the light red streak of blood that was soon washed away by the steady rain.

"No, he's not a Newfie." Carl paused, trying to interject several times before he was able to continue speaking, "Patrick, calm down. He'll get the boat there." He hung up.

Cole asked, "Drugs?"

Carl didn't seem to care. "You'll give them fifty grand, and you bring me back a few bags of pills. Got it?"

Cole nodded. "Simple."

The headlights of a car slowly climbing the curved road up to Cabot Tower pierced the blue morning light. It looped around the lot, slowing as it passed Cole and Carl, then continued on, back down the hill. Cole caught a glance of a young girl sitting shotgun and a boy in his late teens who made every effort to avoid eye contact with both of them. He turned back to Carl. "Young lovers."

Carl had perhaps hoped they'd stop and intervene with whatever plan Cole had devised. He watched as the taillights disappeared back down the hill.

Carl looked at Cole. "Speaking of which, you've been seeing that Olivia girl."

"Leave her out of this, Carl."

He laughed under his breath. "She used to be a cocky little bitch."

Looking away and to his side down a gravel trail leading to the dilapidated stone ruins, Cole nodded towards it, then looked at Carl. "Let's walk."

"Why? It's pissing rain."

Rage building inside, Cole replied, "Daylight is coming. I don't really want to be seen up here with you. And I'd imagine you don't want to be seen either."

"Fuck off. I'm not going anywhere."

Cole pulled the revolver from his shoulder, cocked the hammer, and pointed it squarely at Carl's chest. "Walk, Carl."

"What the hell is that?"

Cole was overcome with a yearning for unchecked violence. He didn't know Olivia's grandfather, but he imagined the man would appreciate Cole for his proper use of it. "Walk, asshole."

He wondered if the rain would soak the percussion caps. If that were the case, he would kill Carl with blunt force trauma. Carl's new expression indicated that he took the revolver seriously, with its long black barrel pointed at him. They made it down the trail to the low stone perimeter of the old pub, nestled on the edge of a steep drop nearly 800 feet to the water below.

"What did you do to Olivia?"

"Is that what this is all about?"

"This is about a lot of things, Carl."

Carl feigned ignorance. "I don't know what you're talking about."

Liar, Cole thought. He pressed on. "And the guns, the drugs?"

Steadying his grip on the gun and pointing it directly at Carl's head, he continued, "You trying to start a war?"

Carl took immediate offense to it, snarling. "Or stop one. The boys have nothing to defend themselves, nothing to fight with. You stand there with a gun in your hand acting like you're too thick in the head to understand?"

"And the drugs?"

Carl looked up for a moment at the sky, then seemed increasingly bothered by the question. "This town could use a little housecleaning. Won't happen with this batch you're bringing back, if that makes you feel any better. The kids get their high, I get some money and the means to bolster the cause back home."

Cole asked, "It's that simple, huh?"

Carl was now pissed. "Yeah. It is that fucking simple."

"And Olivia, how do you know her?"

Carl grinned, sat down on one of the stones, and reached into his chest pocket, fidgeting as Cole pointed the gun at him. "Both hands out there, Carl."

He flared his nostrils, and even through the streaks of caked blood, Cole could see the veins in his neck bulging.

"Hand, Carl, take your *goddammed* hand out."

Carl looked down, speaking to himself. "I should've killed you when I had the chance."

He was pulling something from the inner pocket of his jacket when Cole squeezed the trigger. The hammer dropped and with a muted crack the cap blew, igniting an immediate reaction whereby the powder drove the lead ball out of the barrel towards Carl's chest. Smoke erupted along with a momentary blinding muzzle blast of still-burning black powder. Carl was obscured until the orange flash of powder and grey cloud of smoke disappeared, then slumped over himself.

Cole took two quick steps forward and pushed him backwards, a fifth of Popov vodka falling from Carl's fingers as he looked up at Cole, the rage now softened by the pain, or perhaps the disbelief of having been shot. He breathed heavily and tried to harken some of the meanness for which Cole had known him so well. His chest now opened up, Carl found little strength.

Softly, Carl spoke, "Fuck you," before slumping forward once more and falling to the muddied snow and dead grass at his feet.

Shit, Cole thought. He looked around, unsure of what to do. The irony of these situations was not lost on him, and he drew on his wealth of similar predicaments to think as clearly as his mind would allow. Grabbing Carl by the boots, he dragged him up and out of the small remnants of the long-lost pub's ground floor and farther along the gravel towards the cliff.

Once there, he dug inside Carl's coat pocket, taking his phone and patting him down for any other items of value. Finding none, he unceremoniously rolled Carl's limp body twice until momentum carried him the rest of the way over the cliff. Cole listened for what he thought would be a distant thud, but heard nothing. The sky was now a light shade of grey, and the rain fell harder, omitting any of the colors one might enjoy in a sunrise. Cole edged closer to the ledge and peered down to the water where a moderate swell violently smashed against the cold dark rock, whitewater blasting upwards then back down into the sea. Carl was gone.

Behind him, where he'd shot Carl, the rain was melting away at the snow and left a barely discernable pinkish hue in the snow where Carl's blood had spilled. The grass sticking out from the snow showed just a bit of green, marking what may have been the first true hint of spring. Cole stood for a few moments in the palest of morning light, soaked in the now driving rain, and watched as the last remnants of Carl soaked into the rocky soil of Signal Hill.

Back at the car, Cole sat in the driver's seat and looked behind him at the bloody mess of a backseat. He started it up, backed away from the parking spot, and coasted down the hill, towards town. Tapping the brakes as it rounded a corner, he shifted the car into neutral before bringing it to a stop. Stepping out, he turned the wheel hard to the left and released the brake as it slowly picked up momentum and rolled across the narrow road. Cole hustled next to it with one hand on the wheel. Satisfied it was pointed in the right direction, Cole let go and stopped in the middle of the road as the car continued on, hopped a curb, then crunched across a small gravel walkway and splashed head-on into Deadman's Pond.

It floated slowly in a circle towards the center of the pond. Cole was mildly frustrated that it was taking as long as it did, but he nevertheless watched with patience as Carl's cruiser sunk deeper. At last, she pitched over hard as the open door filled with water, her right quarter pointing upwards as the car rolled on itself and disappeared into the depths. The rain wasn't warm, but neither was it the bitter cold of a winter storm. Cole stood and looked up at the sky, drenched as the rain continued. He smiled as pebble-sized drops bathed his face. The rain was the only sound.

The irony of the pond was not lost on Cole. Rumors abounded of bones laying at the bottom, from centuries past where criminals had been hung or otherwise dispatched. Now Carl's car would join them. It was appropriate, Cole thought, that Carl's death was unceremonious, his body denied even the morbid pomp of a gibbeting that had marked the execution of so many from Newfoundland's storied history. The North Atlantic would carry his remains away, and St. John's would carry on without a second thought.

Tony stared at Cole as he walked in the front door, trepidation in his voice as he asked, "What did you do?"

Cole was busy shucking off his soaking clothes. As he pulled his arm out from one sleeve, he asked, "Did you call the governor yet?"

"No, why?"

Cole dropped his jacket to the floor, then removed the holster from his shoulder. He took Carl's phone from his pocket and wiped it dry with a blanket folded over one of the chairs. Setting it down on the table, he nearly fell as he tried to kick off his boots, a pool of water spilling out from them as he did.

"Carl's gone."

Tony hadn't moved, and Cole tried to avoid looking at him, knowing that Tony's displeasure would only grow.

"What did you do?"

"I killed him."

Tony looked up at the ceiling, then away from Cole and exhaled forcefully, staring then at the far wall. A moment passed before he asked, "Why the hell did you do that?"

"There's more."

"What do you mean?"

"I'm taking that boat tomorrow night."

"Where?"

Cole sat down to pull his pants from his soaked legs. A small pool of water sat on the hardwood floor as he tugged at his socks to get them off as well.

"Dunno. Maybe all the way to Ireland. You wanna come?"

Tony looked directly at him now, not making any attempt to hide his disapproval. "No, Cole. This is too much, even by your standards."

Cole, now down to his boxers, picked up his revolver and walked slowly towards his room. Thinking as he walked, he asked, "You gonna call the governor?"

Tony said, "Not sure yet. Where's Carl now?"

At the doorframe, Cole turned to look at him before replying. "In the Atlantic. His car's at the bottom of Deadman's Pond."

He looked at Tony for a moment more, uncertain if he'd finally lost Tony's support. Tony looked away, only reaffirming Cole's fear. If he'd lost Tony, it was a price he was willing to pay to rid the world of a man like Carl. If there was anything Cole was certain of anymore, it was to not look back on his decisions. Regret served no useful purpose in his life.

Closing the door, he spoke in a low voice. "I need some sleep."

CHAPTER 18: SAYING GOODBYE

LATE IN THE AFTERNOON, Cole retraced his steps from the night before as he approached the *Mary Emmalene*. Wondering if the previous evening hadn't simply been a dream, he half-expected to see Carl laid out on the deck. That thought was interrupted by Matt, who emerged from the wheelhouse and nodded at Cole.

"Can I come aboard?"

Matt nodded and walked back inside. Joining him at a small table on the port side, Cole looked around at the worn interior, its dark paneled walls, and seemingly random bits and pieces of a boat. Matt had the throttle quadrant apart and laid out on a towel, where he'd apparently been tinkering with it until Cole showed up.

"Can I borrow your boat?"

Matt looked at him quizzically. "Where's Carl?"

"Carl's gone. It's just me now."

Matt was clearly smarter than he let on, his mind connecting the pieces of the things he'd seen in the past two days. He was quiet for a moment more before asking, "Will you bring her back?"

He lied. "That's my plan."

Feeling bad for doing so, he followed up, "Do you have insurance?"

Matt laughed quietly, picked up the quadrant cover, and wiped away some grease with a small rag before taking a contemplative breath.

"Yeah, I do."

He looked out the small dirty porthole to his side, then set the quadrant down and shifted his weight to one side, leaning against the bulkhead as he spoke. "There's been times I wish she'd just disappear, and I could make a clean break. But every morning I come down and here she is, just waiting for me."

Cole asked, "The boat?"

Matt laughed. "Yeah, the boat. Cod stocks aren't what they once were. None of my boys want to take on the job. Finding a decent and sober deckhand takes an act of God these days. They're all drunks." He paused, thinking about his words, then continued, "Well, we're all drunks I suppose, but used to be we worked hard anyhow. Not anymore."

"So is that a yes?"

Matt looked at him, his eyes narrowing, as if he might ask for more detail. Instead, he asked once more, "Where's Carl?"

"Gone."

A hint of a smile flickered for a moment on Matt's face before his leathered skin returned to his usual stoic look.

"Yeah, you can have her. Or, 'borrow' her as you said. When?"

Cole nodded in appreciation. "Tomorrow night. Maybe eight or so?"

"You gotta pay for the fuel."

Cole smiled. "Fair enough."

Later in the evening, Cole had found a seat at Green Sleeves, a pint in his hand, listening to Ryan strumming his way through his first set of tunes. Cole let the warm chords soak in as they carried across the floor, Ryan's coarse voice perfectly matched to his mood, and that of another wet evening. The rain had continued all through the day and melted away nearly half of the dirty snow and ice that had laid siege to Newfoundland. By the morning, Cole thought, it may all be gone. Despite the rain, there was talk of spring amongst the patrons in the bar.

Wasting away the next hour, Cole sat and cradled his Guinness in one hand and thought back the past few months. His mind wandered to France and he did nothing to stop it, letting the sullen mood take hold. He'd call tomorrow, before he left, and with a little luck he might be able to talk constructively with Isabella and maybe even Marie.

Wrestling his mind away from her, he heard the house music come on and looked up to see Ryan coming his way.

"Where have you been, friend?"

Cole smiled. "A little busy, but wanted to catch you tonight. How have you been?"

Holding two fingers up to signal a double, he nodded and grinned as the bartender went to work. "I can't complain. The snow's finally melting."

"I may be headed away for a bit."

Ryan took his glass in one hand, spun on his stool to take in the bar scene, and took a small sip before returning his focus to Cole. "For how long?"

"Dunno."

Ryan took a second longer sip, then set the glass down, grimacing as he swallowed a mouthful of whiskey.

"You went all winter in this place and now you're gonna leave right before the weather turns? I'm telling you, Cole, you'll want to be here for the summer. It's gorgeous."

"I'd like to see it."

Ryan spun back around, digging his forearms into the bar and grabbing at his glass to take another sip. "So you and Olivia are a thing?"

Cole laughed and looked away, shaking his head. Taking a long sip from his beer to buy some time and structure his reply, he turned back to Ryan with an honest smile. "How'd you hear that?"

"It's a small enough town. You'd best be careful, though. Every boy in the province is watching you now."

"Is that right?" Cole asked.

Still smiling, Ryan replied, "It is. Is she going with you, wherever you're going?"

The thought of saying goodbye to her troubled him, and Ryan caught the expression on his face, patting Cole firm on the back. "Well, you have to come back now, don't ya? You're a fool if you walk away from a girl like her."

Finishing off his glass, Ryan held it up and rattled the ice in it. "Another set?"

Ryan nodded and grinned. "Story of my life, Cole. Story of my life."

He took his topped-off glass of whiskey as the bartender slid it to him, and Cole rolled his own empty glass in his hand to signal for one more.

"Sticking around?"

Cole nodded. "Yeah, why not."

He took slow sips of two more pints as Ryan played his last set, a few folks now rowdy enough to take to the dance floor. Ryan in turn played even harder to keep the energy building. Cole smiled, seeing St. John's for all that it was. Another night was blossoming, the same good times and mistakes would play out like they always did. The toils of the day would be washed away with stouts and whiskey drinks spilling on the dance floors of George Street. And tomorrow the night would bring more of the same, a gathering of happy folks blissfully unaware as the *Mary Emmalene* slipped out of the harbor.

It was well after ten when Cole finally strolled outside to see that the rain had not deterred anyone from their first temperate night of the year. Perhaps the clouds had dumped the bulk of it already, as only a light mist now hung in the air. It was still cold, just not the piercing winter cold. Looking down the length of George Street, it seemed odd to see bare pavement without the mess of footprints and tire tracks in the slush and ice.

Farther down, at one of the food carts, Cole fixed his eyes on a group of guys gathered around devouring late-night snacks. He was sure they were military. Walking towards them, Cole grinned in earnest when Jake's head popped out from around the group, and he called out to Cole. Seconds later, they exchanged a firm handshake and hug, each of them happy to be catching one another.

"Back for more?"

Jake nodded. "Yeah, got in a couple of hours ago. Fuckers made us do a patrol first, or we would've been in hours ago."

Cole asked, "How's the Atlantic? Still there?"

Jake laughed. "Yup, still there." In a more serious tone, he followed up with another question. "How's the weather out there?"

Jake didn't catch on to Cole's hidden agenda as one of his guys handed him another hot dog bathed in ketchup. He was careful not to spill any on his shirt and answered plainly, "Pretty calm for now. There's supposedly a storm, a big warm front, pushing through in two days."

Cole was quiet as he thought about the implications. Now Jake seemed to sense that he was up to something. He swallowed a big bite and asked, half-jokingly, "You going to sea or something?"

Cole looked at him and nodded. "Yeah, might be."

An hour later, they were both hunkered down at a booth in a dark corner of O'Reilly's, the raucous music from the stage barely audible over the dozens of random conversations taking place throughout the back room. They both sipped at pints of Murphy's as their own conversation wandered its way back to *Delaney*.

"I would've done things different," Cole said as he thought back to what seemed like another life.

Jake replied, "Don't beat yourself up. That boat was absurd. Walters, Potts, they were living in some alternate universe."

"I know, but still, there are times I wish I could've just kept my mouth shut and made it through two years unscathed."

Jake laughed. "Knowing you, man, not a chance."

Cole laughed, too, taking a long sip and looking back over his shoulder at the mayhem closer to the bar. He heard the lazy strokes of a fiddle player and it immediately lifted his spirits, injecting some energy back into his tired conscienceness.

Jake asked, "So seriously, what are you up to tomorrow?"

Cole looked at him, almost certain he didn't want to bring Jake in and risk putting him in any more of a predicament than he already had.

"Nothing major. Just gonna give cod fishing a try."

"Bullshit."

They both laughed and Jake asked, "Can I do anything?'

Cole shook his head, offering a half-hearted, "Nah, but thanks."

After another round of Murphy's, they parted ways after a firm hug, Jake walking backwards into the crowd for a moment to wave once more at Cole before he turned and disappeared down George Street to find his crew. Cole was left alone with his thoughts. It was late enough that he could grab a drink or two with Olivia before she closed up the bar. As he walked towards YellowBelly, he dreaded telling her that he'd be leaving. Hollow promises of being back soon were too much of a lie.

Walking down the stairs, two conflicting emotions tugged at his heart. On one hand there she was, standing behind the bar, yet another one of her dark shirts with long sleeves hanging down from her shoulders. He was immediately struck by her looks, as if he'd never met her in the first place. As he took a seat and he caught her eye, he knew that she'd be disappointed, hurt even, when he told her. Perhaps other people struggled with these same feelings, but still Cole cursed at his predicament and his constantly opposed desires.

With a smile, she asked, "What's got into you?"

He reached out and placed his hand on top of hers, catching the side of her hand with the tips of his fingers. Smiling, he shook his head, "Nothing. Just letting my mind wander."

The clink of several empty glasses on the bar snapped Olivia back to attention, and she walked down the length of the bar to take another order. As she worked on mixing drinks, she slipped a pint down to Cole and winked at him. *Ryan is right*, he thought, admiring the arch of her lower back for the millionth time as she walked back to the other side. Reaching down to grab something under the bar, she tucked her hair behind one ear, and Cole had to tell himself to take a breath. If there was any reason to return, she was it.

Well after one, Cole and Olivia stepped out the back door and into the nighttime air. The rain had finally let go, and they walked together back to her place, stopping a few times to take in views of the harbor and the reflection of ships' deck lights that danced across the narrow stretch of water from one side to the other. Soon enough, they were upstairs in her room, and she played with the collar of his shirt, pulling him towards her. He would tell her, but not just yet, as he didn't want to interrupt the rhythm with which she was removing her own clothes before his. They were soon wrapped up in sheets and each other, breathing heavily and feeding off of each other's desires.

As the intensity peaked, her bed rattled against the wall and with both her hands, she gripped at his disheveled hair and pulled his head down against the side of hers before locking her long legs tight around his waist. He couldn't hold off any longer and as the bed finally settled back down, not quite entirely in the same place where it had been half an hour ago, they both caught their breaths and Olivia pulled a sheet up high over Cole's shoulders, his head falling to a pillow beside hers.

Running her fingers along the length of his arm, she shifted to her side, facing him, and took long slow deliberate breaths, her eyes blinking shut then slowly opening again, as if she was close to sleep.

"Carl's dead."

She turned to face him, her eyes now open and alert, "What do you mean?"

"He's dead. I killed him yesterday."

She thought, unsure of what to think or say. Cole continued, "He's been running this whole thing. The drugs, the boats, the guns. And I called him on it."

Plainly and without judgement, she asked, "Why did you kill him?"

Cole knew not to admit the whole truth, "He would've killed me."

She looked up at the ceiling, and rested her head further into her pillow, as if some weight had been lifted.

"Good." Pausing for a moment, she turned her thoughts to Cole, "Will you get caught?"

Cole smiled just a bit at her, shaking his head, "No, I don't think so."

"Then what will you do now?"

He took a breath and steadied himself, prepping in case the next few moments didn't go well.

"I've got one more thing to handle. I'm going out on a boat tomorrow, to try and knock out the rest of his network."

He watched for her reaction. She did little else but turn a bit more to face him, and he could see the growing concern in her eyes. For so long, he'd felt as if she could see right through him, as if he'd crumble in front of her if she did so much as stare at him for a fraction of a second. But now he saw in her genuine concern over his own well-being. He waited, still thinking that perhaps her eyes would return to their more guarded stance that he'd seen so many times. But as the seconds passed, he wondered if there weren't the smallest of tears clinging to the roots of her long dark eyelashes.

"Where are you going?"

"North, I suppose. Towards Ireland."

Reminding himself that he still needed to make a critical phone call in the morning, he felt his muscles tense up. She must have felt it too, as she stretched her arm across his chest and steadied her own emotions.

"You're coming back?"

There it is, he thought. She'd held her thoughts closely for so long, but now was laying them all out in front of him. *Lie,* he thought, *lie like you always do,* and spare her from the truth. It was a selfish thought and one that he cast aside as quickly as it had affixed itself to his mind.

"I hope so."

He sensed that perhaps she was growing upset with him, and in all likelihood she had the right to.

"What are you going to do?"

"I'm not sure yet."

She looked right through him, and across her small bedroom to the far wall, saying to herself, "I never should've given you that gun."

Cole laughed, thinking that perhaps he'd found a woman that accepted him for who he was, with all his flaws.

She asked, "Did you kill him with that gun?"

"Sure did."

She smiled before trying her best to bury the guilty pleasure she took from Cole's deeds. "Thank you," she said.

Cole took immense satisfaction from her words but dared not press any further. "I can't promise much, but I'll do everything I can to come back here, to you."

She leaned over and kissed him on his mouth, whispering, "You'd better."

CHAPTER 19: TO SEA

IF HE'D SLEPT, it hadn't been for more than an hour or two. Most of the night he was as still as he could be, Olivia's arm or leg, or both, draped over his body and her light breathing against the side of his neck. He stared at the window, knowing that the morning was coming, yet at the same time he wished it wouldn't. As her window was backlit by the first stray bits of waning darkness, he slipped out from under her blanket and made his way downstairs, gathering up what he needed to make a pot of coffee.

Minutes later, as he sat on the couch, he heard her footsteps on the wooden floor above and smiled, thinking to himself about their past few weeks together. Love was too far of a distant thought for him, but Cole felt something for her and knew she felt the same. Her patience while he wrestled with his own emotions impressed him even more. When she came down the steps, she had a pair of his boxers on and an oversized sweatshirt with her hair looped above her head in a barely held-together bun. She was, as always, unintentionally stunning. She smiled and went to the kitchen, took a cup for herself, and sat next to him on the couch, her legs tucked up underneath her as she leaned against his side.

"When are you leaving?"

"Tonight."

They sat in silence for a few minutes, Olivia pretending that she might almost fall asleep again beside him.

"I want to come back here."

She looked at him. "And I want you back here. Be careful, Cole."

"Careful never works."

She looked away. "You scare me when you talk like that."

"If I ever needed a reason to make it home, it'd be for someone like you."

She let out a half laugh. "Is that your way of promising?"

He finished up the last of his coffee and set the cup down on the table beside the couch. "It's the best I can do."

He interlaced each of his fingers with hers and pulled her hand up to his chest, kissing her on her lips. "I need to go."

She walked him to the door and he knew that first fateful step onto her small porch would be the toughest. He hugged her once more, taking a final long breath of what was left of her perfume from the night before, and their eyes locked. Knowing nothing that he could say, he simply smiled and kissed her cheek once more, then turned and hustled down the steps to the sidewalk and picked up his pace to fight the morning chill.

If saying goodbye to Olivia hadn't been enough of a gut punch for the day, he also dreaded parting ways with Tony. As he stepped inside and shucked his jacket off his shoulders, he stopped when he saw Tony at the kitchen table. They looked at each other for a moment more, a sly grin working its way across Tony's face. Spread out on the table was an array of ammunition, guns, and a few random bags.

Cole asked, "Going somewhere?"

With a thud, Tony set an MP5 down on the table, replying, "With you, I guess."

"I didn't think…"

Tony cut him off. "Can't let you go alone. Someone needs to be an adult."

Cole walked slowly across the room, asking, "Do they know back home?"

"I told them it's supposed to be a meeting, not a hit job. Is that a fair assessment?"

Cole shook his head. "No, I'd say that's a lie."

"Then maybe I shouldn't go."

Cole laughed, then backtracked. "Well, they'll be some kind of meeting first..."

Tony picked up a 30-round magazine and began thumbing 9mm rounds into it. "Nothing is black and white, right?"

Cole nodded. "Right."

When he was finished with that one, he grabbed another and began again. Cole went back to his room and emerged with his revolver, setting it down on a rag at the table. Tony stopped loading and asked, "Are you really gonna bring that thing?"

Defensively, Cole replied, "Yeah. Turns out I'm pretty good with it."

He carefully pulled the unspent percussion caps off and removed the barrel and cylinder.

Tony pressed the issue. "Cole, that thing is worthless."

Already cleaning out the one used chamber, Cole looked up and replied, "How many people you killed with that MP5?"

That settled the issue, and Cole went back to cleaning, reloading, and oiling the gun. Once completed to his satisfaction, he held it in both hands, looking it over before tucking it in the holster before he slung it across his shoulder. He then pulled out Carl's phone and flipped it open, pressing the send button. Whichever number came up was the last one Carl had dialed. Cole didn't hesitate to push it again.

A voice on the other end asked, "Hello?"

"Hi. Is this Patrick?"

The thick voice on the other end asked, "Who is this?"

"It's Cole. I'll be heading out tonight to meet you."

"Where's Carl?"

Cole smiled and paused for a moment to add some dramatic flare, "He's dead."

A pause followed, Cole suspecting that Patrick had covered the phone as he could hear some mumbling in the background. Seconds later, Patrick was back on the phone. "Why's he dead?"

"Because he was going to kill me." He paused, for a moment, then added, "Plus he was sloppy. I'll do a better job for you."

"What's your name again?"

"Cole Williams. And you're Patrick, right?"

He paused for some time before replying. "Yeah, I am. So you've got his money?"

"It's my money, and yes, I've got it. Where are we meeting up?"

Patrick said nothing and Cole looked at Tony who was following along with their conversation.

"Patrick?"

Finally, he spoke up. "Thirty west. You head this way, I'll head that way. We'll meet in two days."

Cole nodded, relieved, and said, "That's a plan. I'll be on the *Mary Emmalene*. Red hull. And you?"

"I'll find you," Patrick said before he hung up.

Setting the phone down, Cole looked at Tony and grinned. "I'm pretty fucking good at this stuff."

Tony exhaled, clearly thinking about all the minor details that Cole had not cared to consider. He chewed at his lip for a moment, then spoke. "I think I can get us some satellite coverage. How do you want to handle this?"

Cole shrugged his shoulders. "I dunno. I was thinking we kill them, then come back here for a drink."

Tony looked at him with a stern expression, as if he was a mildly disappointed father, before he said, "I figured that, Cole. But how?"

Cole thought for a moment then said, "Bullets?"

From one of the bags on the table, Tony pulled out what Cole first thought was a kilo of cocaine. He set it down on the table and looked up at Cole as he rolled his fingers across the top of it.

Cole, intrigued, asked, "What's that?"

Tony smiled, "C4." He then produced a second package and set it next to the first. "About four pounds of it."

"So you want to blow them up?"

Tony nodded. "Yeah. Might be easier than shooting it out with them."

Cole agreed. "How do we do that?"

"If we stash it in a bag with the cash and can get it down below, we can remotely detonate it. So long as it's in a confined space, I'd imagine it'll split a boat in half."

Cole's cheeks strained with the smile across his face. "I underestimated you, Tony."

Tony smiled at him. "I know."

Fatigue caught up with him by the afternoon, and he slept for a few solid hours. Packing a small bag, he brought some extra clothes and tucked away the rest of the revolver's supplies in one pocket. He went to work in the kitchen concocting a massive breakfast of all the eggs, bacon, and toast left in the refrigerator. Tony was upstairs and must have caught its scent, because he was soon down as the two of them pushed aside weapons, ammo, and supplies to eat at the big table. Cole pushed one bag and Tony cautioned him, "Careful with that one."

Cole stopped pushing it and with a mouthful, asked, "Why?"

Casually, Tony replied, "I lined that one with the C4."

Cole heard movement upstairs and looked at Tony who simply smiled and turned as a young woman made her way down the stairs. Cole nearly choked when he realized it was the blonde from the governor's office that had refused to even entertain the idea of securing Cole a proper clearance. Her hair was a bit messy, and Cole quickly pieced together what Tony had been up to while he'd been sleeping most of the afternoon.

Tony asked her, "Want some breakfast?"

She looked at Tony, then to Cole, who shrugged and added, "There's plenty."

She politely smiled, hiding any embarrassment quite well and replied, "No, thanks. I should be going." She paused and looked at Tony for a moment, then continued, "Be careful."

As she spoke, she was adjusting her skirt, and Cole couldn't help but grin at Tony, who scowled at him to knock it off.

Standing up, he walked over to her and opened the door, saying, "Thanks" as she cupped his side in a half-hug and walked out. Tony latched the door closed behind her.

"I mean it. I really underestimated you."

Tony shook his head, offering a simple, "Ehh, we've been eyeing each other for a while now."

Cole laughed and finished the rest of his plate, asking, "So she knows about the boat?"

Nodding and taking a seat to finish his food, Tony took a big bite, and answered, "Yeah, the governor is fronting some money."

"How much does he know?"

"I filled him in on most of it."

Cole looked directly at him, asking, "Does he know about Carl?"

Tony smiled to calm his concern, "He knows Carl is dead and didn't care to ask any more about the particular details."

Cole asked, "What does he think?"

"About all of this?"

Tony laughed, put down his fork, and took a breath. He replied, "You mean about drugs, likely from Europe, funneled through Ireland to the streets of Newfoundland, by a crooked cop, to fund weapons shipments from America that may possibly spark a potential civil war?"

Cole thought for a moment, then replied, "Yeah."

"I would imagine he's hoping we can make it go away."

"What do you think about it all?"

Tony shook his head and picked at something stuck between his teeth, unsure of what to say. He didn't move for a few seconds, then shook his head some more, as if he was talking to himself. Clearing his throat, he stumbled for a moment more to find the right words.

"This is some agency-level shit. Like, almost beyond agency-level shit."

He looked at Cole, and joked, "What's with you? This stuff just kind of follows you around the world."

"Makes Panama look pretty vanilla, huh?"

They both laughed.

"Can I borrow the sat phone?"

Tony rummaged through another bag on the table and handed it to Cole, asking, "You calling her?"

Standing up, he replied, "Yeah, probably should."

Outside, he cinched his jacket up around his neck and dialed Isabella's number. It would be the evening in Carentan. Perhaps, Cole thought, Marie would be playing on the rug, Isabella laying on the couch looking for the first signs of her daughter growing tired enough for sleep.

When she answered, Cole paused for a moment before saying a simple, "Hey there."

"Cole?"

"Yeah. How are you?"

He could hear the surprise in her voice and imagined that her mind was racing just as fast as his was.

"I am all right. How are you? Where are you?"

"I'm good, still in St. John's, but I'm heading out for a bit and wanted to talk to you."

"Where are you going?"

He felt the first hint of that same damned tension that had gotten in between them before and knew at that moment that nothing had changed.

"Out on a boat, for a bit."

"And whose dirty work is it this time?"

Her words cut deep, but this time he wasn't mad at her at all for saying them. Before he could even answer, she spoke again, "I'm sorry, that was mean."

"It's all right," he said.

Changing the topic, he shifted the conversation. "How is Marie?"

He hoped with all his heart that Isabella would at least play along and not let the conversation turn toxic.

"She is doing well." Pausing, he could hear Isabella take a breath before she continued, "She is just like you, you know."

It pained him to ask, "Does she remember me?"

"I think she does."

He suspected that was a lie, but it was nice of Isabella to try. He heard her voice in the form of indistinguishable random noises as Isabella played with her. It hurt to hear, but not nearly as much as Cole had expected, or perhaps hoped. The distance had hardened him, and he looked out over the mouth of the harbor, wondering for a moment if he could have done things differently.

"Cole?"

"Yeah?"

"Are you all right?"

"Yeah, I'm fine," he said, refocusing himself on other thoughts. He turned his attention back to her, asking, "How about you?"

"We are fine."

He was looking down at the worn leather of his boots, then to his left at the damp lawn with its hearty green blades of Canada Blue grass that were at last free from the winter snow.

"What will you tell her about me?"

Isabella replied, "That you love her."

He thought for a few seconds about the present and past tense and what would come in the next few days. It was far better that Isabella didn't know. He had to be careful about what to tell her, hoping more than anything that he could end the conversation on good terms.

"You should call more. My father still asks about you."

"I'll try," he lied. "I'm sorry I haven't called in a while."

"It's all right, but if you want to call, you should."

Silence followed, and he wasn't sure what to say. On the line were nothing more than two people who had grown distant, each of them breathing and both likely trying to find a way out of the awkwardness.

She asked, "What are you doing on the boat?"

He thought carefully about his words. "Trying to fix something."

That didn't do any justice to sum up the complexity of the past few weeks. He turned the focus back to his little girl. "Will you tell her that I was a good person?"

"You are a good person, Cole."

He'd inadvertently slipped to the past tense and winced at his mistake, replying, "Thanks."

"She's lucky to have you," he said.

"Why are you talking like that?"

He knew without a doubt that it was time to end the call.

"No reason, but I should go. Tell her that I love her." He thought for a moment about how he felt about Isabella. It wasn't love, as that hope had already faded. Unsure of how to end it, he said simply, "I'll call again if I get a chance."

Before Isabella could reply, he mashed down the red button to end the call and sat upright, leaning against the door, setting the phone down in his lap. He sat there for a few moments, clenching his fists to warm up his fingers and taking rhythmic breaths of the crisp air until his nerves settled and he walked back inside.

CHAPTER 20: NORTH BY EAST

COLE WATCHED WITH an odd kind of numbness as Tony locked the door, turned, and walked towards his already-running truck. Climbing in to the driver's seat, he asked if Cole was ready. Cole nodded, as if there were other options still on the table. As Tony started down the road, away from the Battery, Cole leaned forward in his seat to take one last look at their house's orange paint. The final defiant streaks of yellow from a fading sun left the house almost glowing behind them. With a quick turn on the narrow road it was gone, and Cole pressed his head back against the headrest, trying not to think of anything but the task at hand.

Tony parked in a gravel lot near the wharf, and paused, looking at the keys and clearly wondering what to do with them. Tucking them in his pocket, he left it unlocked as both of them slung heavy bags over their shoulders and walked another 50 yards towards the water. Quietly tied up to rusted cleats, *Mary Emmalene* seemed to be waiting for them in peace. Cole dropped his bag and hopped over the low gunwale to the wooden deck and turned for Tony to hand him the bags. Once onboard, Cole took a few steps and peered inside the cabin, where he was surprised to see the governor. Matt was seated across from him, holding a bag across his lap.

"Tony, you may want to come over here."

Walking over, Tony looked inside, then turned to Cole to confirm that he, too, was unsure of the unfolding situation.

"Come on in," the governor said.

Once they were all seated around the cramped table, the governor cleared his throat and spoke first. "I've gone ahead and paid Matt here for his boat."

Matt looked at both Cole and Tony with the first hint of uncertainty they'd seen from him.

The governor continued, "You two know what you're doing?"

Cole answered, "Yes, Sir. I think we do."

He looked for a few moments more at the two of them and took a long breath before shifting in his seat. "I can't do much for you. Canada doesn't have the stomach for these kinds of things. Tell me, Tony, I wonder if the U.S. does?"

Tony replied, "Sir, we're walking a fine line. The truth isn't as black and white as would be necessary to answer your question. We'll be mostly on our own."

He looked at Tony, absorbing the magnitude of what he'd just said. A moment later he turned to Cole, and said, "Thank you then to both of you. I'm afraid we've gotten ourselves into quite a mess."

Tony assured him, "We'll do what we can to shut this network down."

Cole cut in. "This one, we'll stop." He paused and looked at the governor before continuing. "The next one may be on you, Sir."

The governor nodded. "Always a next one, isn't there?" He continued, "If I may ask, what happened to Carl?"

Matt shifted in his seat and the wooden slats beneath it creaked. Cole looked at him just as Matt turned to look outside and ignore whatever followed.

"He won't be causing any more trouble, Sir." Cole answered.

The governor asked, "Did he really orchestrate this whole thing?"

"It looks that way," said Tony.

"Damn shame. His parents were good people," the governor said. He then shifted out from his seat and stood in the dark and damp passageway, brushing off some water from his jacket.

"Take care of yourselves," he said, unsure beyond that what to say. With a sudden awkward pivot, he turned and stepped out from the hatch, onto the deck, and disappeared. Matt stood up next, clutching his bag of cash.

To Cole, Matt said, "She's not the fastest, but she's got enough muscle to pull half the ocean up." He took a breath and exhaled slowly, looking at both of them before he continued. "There's a storm in a day's time. You know that?"

Cole nodded. "I know."

"The hull is solid; she'll take care of you. I've tended to that engine for twenty years. Don't take her beyond six-thousand RPM unless you need to. You'll burn her up."

"Thanks," was all Cole said, filing that away in the back of his mind.

He extended his hand to shake Matt's. With a firm leathered palm, Matt gripped his hand and shook it hard before he too disappeared into the night, leaving Cole and Tony by themselves.

"Well, fuck it," Cole said as he fired up the old diesel engine and listened to her grudgingly come to life. He could feel the engine under his feet, a rhythmic hum that settled as it warmed up. Walking out on the aft deck, he took a long breath of the exhaust that floated up from the transom and drifted with the night breeze. He walked across to the port rail and cast off the stern line before quickly hopping up onto the rail and around the wheelhouse to let go of the bow line as well.

Back inside, he clutched ahead, and she pivoted smartly on the spring line. With a groan and a few clicks, she settled back in neutral, her stern swinging out further.

"Let go of that spring line, Tony."

He asked, "You want me to get it from the wharf?"

Cole thought for a moment before replying, "Doubt we'll need it where we're going."

Tony untied it from the *Mary Emmalene's* cleat and let if fall into the dark water, churning from the propeller wash below them.

Cole reversed her farther out into the harbor, and once clear of the other boats that sat dark and still against the wharf, he clutched ahead once more and spun the wheel, pointing the bow towards the mouth of the harbor. The sun was now gone, a vivid blue light streaking across the western horizon behind them. The air was calm and cold. Cole worked one of the portholes open to take in some fresh air against the stagnant smell of two decades' worth of Matt's cigarettes.

Tony stayed out on the deck, leaning against the starboard gunwale and looking towards the town. Cole also couldn't help but look to his left at St. John's. He thought about George Street, then Olivia. She was at the UnderBelly, no doubt mixing a drink for some jolly fool. He wondered if she was thinking about him at the same moment. He found himself consumed with more intimate thoughts and the particulars of her skin against his and the warmth of her bed.

Gritting his teeth, he stared forward at the harbor mouth. *Enough of that*, he told himself. Pushing the throttle up some more, at 2,000 RPM the *Mary Emmalene* pushed along at nearly eight knots. As they approached the narrow mouth, Tony stepped inside and took a seat on the port side, looking out a window at the towering cliffs. Cole's thoughts centered on the two he'd killed in this same spot and his battle to stay alive as he swam for the same cliffs that now passed by silently.

They unceremoniously passed the mouth, and the *Mary Emmalene* rocked gently with the ocean swell that rolled in from the south.

Cole asked, "Can you take her for a bit?"

Tony looked surprised, unsure of what that meant. Cole smiled. "Take the wheel, keep her on a zero eight zero heading. I'm just gonna catch some fresh air."

Tony shrugged and walked over, placing one hand on the stainless wheel and squinting his eyes towards the magnetic compass in front of him. Cole walked aft, past the table, then through the hatch to the open deck. He continued to the transom and sat down on the port quarter, one leg hanging over the side. He pulled the collar of his jacket up high around his neck then dug his hands deep into his pockets and tight against his torso.

He looked aft, at the fading sliver of St. John's that was still visible between the dark rock cliffs. The boat took several wandering turns and Cole laughed out loud, envisioning Tony's discomfort with the subtleties of reading a dimly lit magnetic compass. Another turn followed, and Cole's entire body was shaking with laughter. He called out, "Get it under control, Tony."

A muffled voice replied, "Fuck you, Cole."

Several hundreds yards to the north, where the cliffs reached nearly 800 feet, he wondered if he could pick the spot where Carl's body likely lay. He narrowed his gaze and chewed at his lip, remaining there for some time as the ominous black coast of Newfoundland disappeared beneath the horizon, leaving only the deep Atlantic beneath him and the stars in the sky above. *What is it about the sea*, he wondered. He had missed Olivia terribly just an hour before, but now on the open sea, his mind shifted to the many tasks at hand that would keep him busy until he made landfall again, if ever. For that, he was thankful.

Back inside, he stood next to Tony for a moment, who huffed with frustration. Cole laughed again and offered to take the first watch.

He spent the night at the helm, slowly getting a feel for the old boat and how she gently rolled with the quartering seas. *A good boat doesn't fight the waves*, he thought. With time, Cole could let her drift with the passing swells and give her just enough rudder to settle her back on course each time. The engine hummed along peacefully, giving Cole time to think as his mind wandered back and forth with thoughts of Newfoundland.

———

It was after six in the morning when the first faint light pierced the eastern horizon, first as a subtle blue, then the familiar streaks of yellow and orange that gave away the sun's impending rise. He managed to get a pot of coffee going in the wheelhouse, no doubt the coffeemaker having been tactically positioned by Matt to keep him awake for days on end of cod fishing. It was a hardy roast that Cole had scooped out from an old plastic container and as he took his first sip, he smiled. The sleepless

night had been worth the sunrise that he now admired with near solitude. Tony was up soon after, having no doubt smelled the coffee wafting aft to the bench where he'd slept.

"You want to get some rest?"

"Sure," Cole replied as he stepped aside and Tony rested his hands
on the wheel again. At a chart on the table, Cole plotted their position
once more against a line he'd drawn between St. John's and Westport.
They were a bit south for Cole's liking and he called out, "Give it about
a zero seven five."

Tony nodded, and Cole stepped aft to take a leak off the stern. As
he exited the hatch, he looked back to the west at the darkness and
stared, thinking that perhaps there was something lurking in the western night. He finished his cup of coffee and waited. Twenty minutes
passed as the blue light crept over his head and marched steadily westward. He looked away, then back to confirm his fears. Above him the
sky was clear, but not far to the west there were unsettled low clouds
spinning and colliding against themselves as they marched east.

Back in the wheelhouse, Tony turned and looked with surprise. "I
thought you'd be asleep by now."

Cole poured himself another cup of coffee. "That storm's creeping
up on us. I'm gonna get everything secured."

Tony looked forward again, at the compass, then slowly around at
the wheelhouse, its worn wooden panels, then down at the stained and
soiled rugs. Cole felt the same kind of uncertainty, but he dared not
show it. Tony would be better off if Cole kept calm. He crawled down
to the engine room with a flashlight and peered around at the sides of
the old diesel engine. It was uncomfortably warm, but the space was
mostly dry, telling Cole that Matt had not lied to him. From there, he
was out on the main deck again where he tied down the random boat
hooks, buckets, and coiled lines. Once done, he looked west once more
and saw the first white caps rising up in the distance from the otherwise
grey plane of a calm morning sea.

Back inside, he dogged down the hatch and double-checked each of the portholes in the small galley. Finally, he walked back up to the wheelhouse and to the porthole he'd opened the night before. Just as he did, a new breeze filled in, colder than the one he'd felt all night. The air swirled around him just as he closed it and dogged it down.

Tony asked, "Is it bad?"

Cole replied, "Yeah. We're in for a long day."

An hour later, Cole was at the helm, struggling to keep her on any course for more than five seconds. Raindrops pelted the windows like stones and made it all but impossible to see the confused sea state all around. Time and again, Cole was blindsided by a swell against the beam and whitewater ran over the bow, heeling the *Mary Emmalene* uncomfortably to her port side, where Tony sat, his foot pressed firmly against the console in front of him to keep from falling out. Cole spread his feet and worked the engine unsuccessfully to find a more comfortable ride. He took evenly spaced breaths, remembering his many runs through the Caribbean on nights like these.

His mind wandered to a different sea, where the water had been warm and the storms characterized by wild lightning and booming thunder that roared down on him. Here, in the North Atlantic, the storm felt different, as if the wind collided against the hull and shook the wheelhouse with unchecked rage. Even in the lulls, it still hit hard and fast. Looking to the radar, it was nothing more than a solid return of green, with no end in sight. She rolled hard with another passing swell, and Cole swore that the starboard side had been submerged by a solid wave that washed over the deck and wheelhouse. Still, the *Mary Emmalene* pressed on, the hum of her engine long ago drowned out by the incessant howling wicked wind.

Back by the galley, something heavy fell with a thud, and Tony looked at Cole to see if he should go investigate.

"Leave it," Cole said, and he refocused on the spinning compass. Two hours later, the storm intensified, and Cole could feel it shifting north and east. The confused swells now had more east in them than before, and the *Mary Emmalene* rolled through the deep troughs as best she could. Cole guessed that they were in 30-foot seas. She'd dig in to the bottom of a swell then launch herself upward and over the top where the stern was likely lifted up and out of the water. He could feel the shudder of the propeller as it clawed through the air trying desperately to dig back into the water. Each time a swell passed, Cole lost forward momentum and fought hard to keep any control over the wildly swinging bow. He was running on adrenaline at this point, half his efforts focused on keeping her on course and the other half drifting with random scattered thoughts as fatigue worked its way further into his mind. For a moment, he was in Olivia's bed before he felt himself falling forward and shook his head to wake himself and find something on which to focus.

"At least we're dry," he said to Tony.

Reluctantly, and over the pelting rain and driving wind, he replied, "Yeah, I guess so."

Cole smiled and turned his efforts back to the compass. Another three hours passed, and Cole was growing confident that they'd weathered the worst of it. Riding out a storm was a marathon and not a sprint. Twice since the winds had turned north, he'd poured himself more coffee and held it with one hand to keep the cup from spilling. What he needed was some food, but there was no chance of that right now. He looked over to Tony, who still sat with his foot pressed against the console. Scratching his head, Cole wiped his heavy eyes and knew that he wouldn't make it much longer.

"Tony, can you take her for a while?"

Tony looked at Cole, then reluctantly nodded and steadied himself with both feet on the deck. Hand over hand, he crossed the cramped wheelhouse and took the helm.

Cole instructed him, "Just keep her headed a bit north of east. A few more hours and I think we'll be out of this."

Tony yelled, "Where are you going?"

Cole looked at the far corner of the wheelhouse and pointed at the deck, saying, "Right there. Wake me if you need me."

Tony nodded, then peered ahead, looking for anything beyond the incessant rain that poured down on top of them. Cole stumbled aft and grabbed an oily blanket from the galley. He worked his way forward again, checking on Tony once more before sliding over to the port side and laying down on the cold deck. He balled the blanket up and tucked it under his head. Within moments, he was asleep.

His eyes closed, he heard the familiar hum of the diesel engine but nothing else. The boat rolled gently, and he opened his eyes to see Tony leaning against the captain's chair, one hand on the wheel. There was no more rain, and Cole needed a few moments to process his surroundings. His left leg was numb from sleeping on his side, and he struggled to stand up as Tony looked at him and laughed.

"How long was I out?"

Tony smiled, then looked back forward and checked his heading. "A little over five hours."

"Well, fuck. I needed that."

He went to plot their position and despite the storm, little more than a small correction was needed. "Bring it north again, Tony. Another five degrees."

"Zero seven zero, aye, Captain."

Cole looked at him. Tony just laughed and Cole finally did the same. Back in the galley, Cole dug through the reefer for some food and was able to rustle up some bread and a stick of butter. In the oven he heated up what was left of a sliced loaf of bread and brought it up to Tony where they slathered the entire stick on warm toast and devoured it. Splitting a gallon of water between them, Cole nodded to himself, now certain they'd survived the storm.

They steamed east under a thick blanket of fog that hung no more than five or ten feet above the surface of the sea.

Tony said, "This stuff looks pretty thick."

Cole replied, "Yeah. Might be with us for a while. Why?"

"No reason, just thinking those satellites can't see through this stuff."

Cole nodded. "We'll manage. You mind if I step out for a bit?"

"Nah, go for it. I'm good for a while."

Cole walked aft, stopping to check that the engine room was in fact still dry. Out on the back deck, he was pleased that nothing had been lost overboard. Peeking up and over the wheelhouse, it appeared that the superstructure hadn't been damaged either. The deck and railing were wet, and with a heavy fog, they wouldn't dry anytime soon. Cole ran his fingers along the railing until they were soaked with water then rubbed them hard against his face, tasting the fresh water on his lips. He could practically reach up and touch the fog. In all directions, the sea was grey, as if all the varied colors of the ocean had been carried away by the storm. Another night would soon pass, and Cole hoped that he'd see the sun once more when it was finally over.

CHAPTER 21: THE BATTLE

THE NIGHT PASSED uneventfully. On a calm sea, the *Mary Emma-lene* had made good speed, and they neared the rendezvous as midday approached. Tony had laid out an arsenal, picking tactical locations around the main deck from which the two of them could have decent cover and fight if need be. Across the table in the wheelhouse, he'd set down two M4s and a mess of magazines. Aft in the cramped galley were two more guns and spare magazines. On the aft open deck were more tucked in between a holding tank and the bulkhead where still more magazines were stuffed into the crevices.

Cole was at the wheel, scanning ahead as best he could in the half mile or so of visibility. The fog was no more than 100 feet above them, its thick haze not allowing even a hint of sunlight to push through. Cole knew that without even the slightest lighter shade above them, the fog would not lift anytime soon. They greyness of the sky was paired perfectly with the sea, and the thin stretch of horizon all around was only a shade or two lighter, giving some illusion of being in a universe devoid of anything.

Above the hum of the engine, he could hear the occasional wave of whitewater crumble ahead of the bow. With the portholes open, Cole took a deep breath of the Atlantic air and thought back to the fisheries patrols he'd done onboard *Delaney*. They'd never ventured this far north or east, though, and he enjoyed the thought of new waters. Halfway to Ireland, there was an immense and heavy feeling of solitude that Cole relished. He found it calming, as if there was finally enough space and freedom for him to think with a clear mind. Leaving St. John's had been tough, but now, with nothing around him and on the open sea, Cole was once again content. Wrapping his hands around the wheel and gripping tight, he let a smile escape.

"What are you smiling about?"

Looking back at Tony, he laughed. "Just enjoying this."

"The ocean, or the fight in front of us?"

He thought for a moment before replying. "Both, I guess."

Tony set a cup of coffee next to Cole then took a seat on the port side and threw one leg up high against the chart table. He took a sip and stared straight ahead.

"If you can get that bag down below, get it near the hull and in an open space that'll flood quick. We can trigger it with this remote."

Cole looked over to see that Tony had what appeared to be a garage door opener in his hand. He set it carefully on the chart table amidst the pile of 30-round magazines.

Cole asked, "You think we'll need all this?"

"Hope not."

"Is all the money in the bag?"

"Yup."

Cole grinned. "Anything else you had smuggled away in that house that I should know about?"

Tony looked at him with a sly grin and said nothing. Cole turned his attention back to the radar and an intermittent blip about seven miles out ahead of them. He tapped his finger against the screen and nodded. "That might be them."

Tony stood up and walked over, rubbing his hands through his disheveled hair. He then finished his cup of coffee and asked, "How long?"

"Maybe half an hour."

Tony took the first M4 and pushed a magazine in until it clicked. Pointing it down towards the deck, he pulled back the charging handle then released it with a clink of the spring inside the buffer tube. He did the same with the second one then pulled the bolt back once more to confirm that a round was loaded. Cole still had his pistol slung across his chest and he touched his fingers against the wooden grip, adjusting it slightly.

"You're not really gonna use that thing, are you?"

Defensively, Cole replied, "Yeah, I might."

"Cole, please be serious about this."

"I'm batting one hundred with this, Tony. It's good luck."

Expressionless, Tony stared at him. He set a Sig 226 down on the table and spun it until the muzzle was pointed forward.

"Mine's cooler," Cole quipped.

The visibility had opened up to nearly a mile, but still under a thick overcast layer, Cole could see nothing ahead as he steamed onward. The radar blip became more and more consistent as they closed to within four miles. Tony stepped aft to check on his cache of ammo and weapons once more.

Cole asked, "Got any grenades?"

Tony looked at him. "No."

He paused, then said, "Matt said you really took a liking to them in Mexico."

Cole laughed, then replied, "Harley's fault."

Tony leaned against the chart table, his voice now a bit more solemn. "He was a stud, that's for sure."

Cole cleared his throat. "Did you ever hear about how he nearly drowned while we were spearfishing?"

Tony shook his head. "No, never heard that."

"Matt had to drag him back up, all because of a damn grouper."

Tony laughed. "That sounds like Harley." He paused for a moment, then asked, "How'd it turn out?"

"Matt got him breathing again, then we ate tacos that night on the beach."

They were silent for a few moments, both of them thinking their own thoughts and staring out at the vast grey expanse in front of them, the *Mary Emmalene* rocking gently from side to side as a small swell rolled in from the north. For Cole, it was uncomfortably calm, serene even, as he leaned against the seat behind him, one hand on the wheel, and the diesel-tainted cool breeze swirling about the wheelhouse.

Matt's elbow had worn part of the padded armrest down to the wood, and Cole ran his index finger around its small circular outline. "You mind taking the wheel for a bit?"

Tony took a glance at the compass and walked over. Cole stepped aft and out onto the open deck to have a few final moments by himself. He took long deep breaths of the air on the port side and leaned against the railing, looking at the wake trailing off behind him. It spread out in a shallow V shape, dark lines of the small waves trailing off in either direction. Cole rubbed his hand against his chin and thought about death. He was far calmer than he'd been in Panama, or even Mexico. He was perhaps at last well prepared for what was to come. If he was going to die, his would be an anonymous death, like so many other men over the centuries who had taken to the sea to find their destiny.

Perhaps another pistol, he thought, before smiling to himself and re-committing to the old six-shooter. Once he'd expended the six lead balls loaded in its cylinder, perhaps then he'd upgrade to the 21st century. Tony would no doubt lay down enough covering fire for whatever was in store. He tried to think of Marie, but found it difficult, his mind hardened for the time being and focused on the task at hand. Walking aft, he leaned against the transom and looked down at the churning white water below. Cole stood motionless for another half minute, then turned and walked back into the wheelhouse.

Tony seemed calm, having learned over the past two days how to keep the old boat on course with minimal corrections. When left alone, the *Mary Emmalene* had a way of finding her own track, like any good boat. He walked over and stood next to Tony, seeing the solid radar return now only three miles ahead of them.

Cole watched for a few seconds, running a plot in his mind, and remarked, "They've turned towards us."

Tony just nodded. They steamed onward for another ten minutes, Cole squinting and staring ahead just off of their port bow, looking for the first signs of the target. A minute later, he felt chills run down his back. Fighting the slightest twinge of nerves, he exhaled hard and pointed. "There."

"What do you want me to do?"

"I'll take the wheel."

Cole slid over and gripped the wheel with one hand and draped the other over the throttle. He turned her to starboard as the dark hull came into view a half mile in front of them. The two boats closed to within 100 yards, and Cole could see two men on the back deck. She was a fishing boat as well, roughly the same size as the *Mary Emmalene*. Cole throttled back to two or three knots and crept closer. They circled each other once, as if jockeying about to line up for a broadside with the wind in their favor.

Cole turned the *Mary Emmalene* harder to port and approached the port side of the other boat. He couldn't see inside the wheelhouse, but there were two men standing on the port side, staring at him as Cole approached.

"Can you go tie us off?"

"Sure," Tony replied as he tucked the Sig into the small of his back and flipped his shirt over to conceal it.

With a slight bump, Cole nudged the starboard bow against the other boat then brought the clutch to neutral. He took a deep breath and pulled his jacket on over his shirt, then zipped it halfway up to conceal his pistol. Walking aft, he grabbed the bag of cash and stepped through the hatch out onto the deck. It was heavier than he remembered, and he caught Tony looking at him with a faint grin.

As Cole approached, he whispered, "I doubled the charge." With a wink, he then continued, "Just to be certain."

Tony then stood back and Cole surmised that no one had yet spoken.

From the deck of the *Mary Emmalene*, he called out, "Patrick?"

The two on the other boat looked at Cole for a moment. They were both thin but mean, Cole sensing that neither were going to let their guard down. Their clothes were ragged and soiled, leaving Cole to wonder if there were in fact perhaps fishermen.

He asked again, "Is Patrick onboard?"

One of them motioned down below with a slight nod of his head. Cole stepped forward and took a breath to steady his nerves. At the rail, with the bag in one hand, he hopped over and onto the deck of their boat. Neither of them men moved much, one standing on each side of him.

"Down below?"

The taller of the two answered with a grunt from his closed mouth. Cole looked over to the small wheelhouse and started walking. Once inside, he smelled the thick raw smoke of unfiltered cigarettes. He stepped down a small ladder, and his eyes quickly adjusted to the darkness. At an empty table against the hull sat two men, both staring back up at Cole.

"Patrick?"

One of them, with long jet black and matted hair, nodded. "And you're Cole?"

Taking a seat on a thin and barely held-together cushion, he tried to smile and replied, "Yeah. Nice to meet you."

Farther forward was another three steps that led up to the helm. Cole could see only the feet of whomever was at the helm, and then a shadow moved from the other side. In his mind, he counted five total, thinking to himself of the odds for him and Tony. Against the far side was an FAL rifle. Cole looked at it for a moment before Patrick spoke, "It's a FAL."

"I'm familiar with them," he said before turning to face Patrick once more.

Shifting in his seat, Cole pulled the bag across his lap and set it between him and the hull. He looked at both of them, then asked, "So you've got something for me?"

Patrick nodded at the other guy who got up and went over to a cabinet where he pulled out a backpack and unzipped it, looking to Patrick for his cue. Cole stared at each of them, then unzipped his bag and began laying out the banded rolls of cash on the table. Patrick picked up two of them and unrolled them, thumbing through the bills.

He then set them down and asked, "What happened to Carl?"

"He tried to kill me."

"So you killed him?"

Cole nodded. "Yeah. I mean, that's an abbreviated version, but yeah."

"So now we should trust you?"

Cole let his lip curl with a bit of a smile, and replied, "Should I trust you?"

Patrick said nothing, staring at Cole. Looking over at the guy with the backpack, then back at Patrick, Cole was cautious not to push too far.

"What happened with that last batch of pills?"

Patrick shrugged. "Bad mix, I guess."

Cole nodded at the guy with a backpack, "And that one?"

Patrick sat back and answered, "Pretty sure they've worked out the kinks." He quickly followed up by asking, "Can you get guns?"

"I'm American."

Patrick, now seemingly frustrated, asked, "What's that supposed to mean?"

Cole laughed. "Yeah, I can get you guns. Rifles?"

Patrick replied, "Or pistols, ammo, magazines, whatever."

"You trying to start a civil war?"

Patrick leaned forward and snarled, "None of your goddamned business."

Cole put both of his hands up to ease the tension. "I didn't mean anything by it." He looked over at the bag and asked, "We good?"

Patrick nodded as Cole set out the last of the rolls of money and the other guy brought the backpack over and set it in front of Cole. Inside was a gallon-sized zip-locked bag of bright yellow pills. With one hand, Cole reached over to it, and opened it further to look inside. With his other hand, he reached for the now-empty bag of cash and set it down by his feet, sliding it under the table and against the hull.

"Well, all right then. I'll be in touch."

He was nervous as he turned his back to Patrick and the other guy. If they were going to kill him, now was the time. As he stepped up onto the deck, he felt beads of sweat on his chest and under his armpits. Taking a deep breath, he walked casually over past the two guys on deck and hopped over the railing to Tony. In his hand, Cole could see the remote detonator. He nodded at Tony, who clicked the button.

Nothing happened. They looked at each for a moment in disbelief, unable to speak outside of hearing distance from the other two. Cole had his back to the two men on the boat. He looked at Tony for a second, set the backpack down, then reached slowly with his right hand to retrieve his revolver. Tony stared at him as if to say no, but before he could, Cole was spinning and cocking the hammer. In an instant, he aimed instinctively at the closer of the two and let loose a cloud of smoke with the familiar blast of unburnt powder spewing from the barrel. The first guy fell where he stood and the second ran around the far end of the wheelhouse, disappearing before the smoke had cleared.

"Give me the remote," Cole yelled as he snatched it from Tony's hand and jumped over the railing back onto the other deck. From the wheelhouse, someone opened up with a barrage of fire and Tony was quick on his feet with an M4 firing back in three round bursts. Cole turned to see that Tony had a solid position to lay down some covering fire. Lunging forward toward the hatch leading below, Cole was met by the one from below coming up the small steps with the FAL. In an instant, Cole cocked the hammer again and fired from a low draw into the man's gut. He fell backwards and slumped down on the deck below, rolling and crying out in pain. The smoke masked his view until the flash of a muzzle caught his attention.

The shot missed, but Cole turned to take cover as someone emptied a magazine in his direction. It was a pistol, of that much he was certain. After what must have been 12 or 14 rounds, Cole guessed they were reloading and turned once more, firing into the cramped cabin before the same gunman opened up with a second magazine. Cole exposed his right hand in the corner of the hatch with the remote and mashed down the button once more. In an instant, his hand felt the heat first, then the concussive blast from below. The whole boat shuddered, and the air seemed to swell from the explosion. Bits of wood and debris flew out from the hatch and Cole's ears hurt badly.

Crouched now beside the hatch, he looked over at Tony and the two made eye contact.

Tony yelled, "You good?"

Cole moved his jaw in a circle to try and ease the ringing in his ears then slowly nodded, his senses not yet fully recovered. Tony dropped the magazine from his rifle and slammed another in.

"Come on," he yelled.

Cole stood up into a low crouch and took quick steps across the deck. As he did, someone appeared from the wheelhouse and took a shot at him. Feeling the disturbed air from a passing bullet, Cole ducked back and looked as Tony opened up with more three round bursts. Cole stood once more and sprinted across the deck, leaping up and over the railing before falling to the deck of the *Mary Emmalene* as spent cases from Tony's rifle rolled about in random directions.

"Keep on them," he yelled as Cole hopped up and ran forward to the wheelhouse.

Tony was firing relentlessly from the deck, pausing for a few seconds at a time, no doubt burning through magazine after magazine. Once he was at the wheel, he yelled back, "Cut her loose, Tony."

Cole put the *Mary Emmalene* into reverse and backed away. Once he was about 20 yards out, he looked up and saw someone emerge from the wheelhouse and point a rifle at him. Cole had spun her in such a direction that he'd blocked Tony's line of fire. Cursing at himself, Cole ducked just as the other boat opened up with automatic fire. The windows shattered as bits of glass and wood splinters flew all over the wheelhouse and down Cole's back. Whoever was firing had dumped an entire magazine at him, but Cole was unhurt. He stood up once more as Tony was running in to cover him.

Cole peeked over the now-shattered chart table and could see that the other boat was listing at least five degrees to starboard. Someone opened up again, and Tony met their rate of fire with one of the MP5s. More bullets tore through the wood paneling in the wheelhouse as more splinters flew wildly about. Tony stood in the line of fire until he'd emptied his magazine. He dropped down to reload, and Cole peered up again, unable to control the ridiculous grin on his face. He throttled ahead, the bow pointed directly at the port side of the other boat. Cole mashed the throttled down and the *Mary Emmalene* shuddered uncontrollably.

Tony asked, "What are you doing?"

"Their hull is split. I'm gonna ram them."

He pressed the throttle and saw the muzzle of a rifle appear from a dark porthole.

"Hold on," Cole said calmly.

A moment later the *Mary Emmalene* smashed into the side of the other boat, slamming both Tony and Cole forward. The engine was groaning from down below, and Cole stood up to see that he'd hit her midships and was now heeling her over further to starboard. He stood, cocked the hammer of his revolver with one smooth motion, and fired again as the smoke enveloped both him and Tony for a few seconds. Tony was up and firing. Cole cocked the hammer, firing at nothing in particular and Tony yelled at him, "Cole, fucking quit that."

Cole ignored him and fired again until the revolver was empty, at which point he calmly set it down and admired the dirty brass trigger guard. He backed away a good 30 or 40 yards and could see that the other boat was badly damaged. Spinning the wheel, he positioned the *Mary Emmalene* for a *coup de gras*. The blast had punctured her hull on the port side, and the boat was beginning to roll further to her side now as the hull flooded with water.

"Ah, shit," Tony said with reluctance as Cole looked up to see the gaunt frame of someone aiming a rocket at them from the mortally wounded boat. Tony was shouldering his rifle as the thin wisp of smoke spiraled towards them from the other boat. Cole and Tony dove to the deck, falling amongst the shards of glass, busted wood, and bits of debris that littered the deck. The rocket struck low at the *Mary Emmalene's* waterline, rattling both of them. Cole popped up to see smoke rising from her bow. He mashed the throttle once more and built speed slowly. Nearing six knots by the time he struck the other boat again, he hit her hard and kept on with all the torque he could muster. Matt had been right as the *Mary Emmalene* drove hard into the hull a second time. The deck shook violently and Cole suspected he was pushing her too far. At the same time he feared there was no hope in saving her with what must have been a gaping hole in her own bow.

The engine strained harder as he rolled the other boat nearly 45 degrees to starboard. After nearly half a minute, he backed down and could see an enormous gash in her port side. The boat steadied for a moment and Tony emptied another 30-round magazine into the wheelhouse for good measure. As he dropped the magazine and loaded another, the boat rolled hard to port before the stern dropped quickly below the waterline and the bow began to rise. She was sinking.

From the rail, one man jumped overboard as the bow rolled further to port and pointed nearly vertically as air blew violently out from an open forward hatch. Within seconds the boat was gone, leaving only a scattered debris field among a sheen of oil and fuel. One man swam, his arms taking wild strokes towards them. Cole picked up an unused M4 from what was left of the chart table, shouldered it, and took a solitary shot, striking the man in his head.

Tony looked on as the lifeless body slowly submerged and disappeared. "What now?" he asked.

Cole set the rifle down and replied, "We better get the life raft."

CHAPTER 22: A RUMBLE IN THE DISTANCE

THEY SAT ACROSS from each other, neither having made it into the raft entirely dry. What little supplies they'd grabbed would last for a few days if they were careful and rationed the water. Cole's legs were soaked from his thighs on down, and Tony wasn't in much better shape. The *Mary Emmalene* had gone down quickly. Cole reasoned that even without a hole punched in her bow from the rocket, the engine never would have made it back to Newfoundland after the beating it had taken. But, as he played games in his head, he thought that the boat would have been a far better choice than an old life raft to weather the North Atlantic.

The same persistent low fog still hung over them as the afternoon wore on. Tony was quiet for most of it, shivering as he sat and stared across the flat sea. The grey light was slowly turning darker as the evening approached. Cole doubted they'd make it through the night.

Finally, Tony asked, "Why aren't you shivering anymore?"

Cole looked at him. "How much do you know about hypothermia?"

Tony looked away, unwilling to accept what Cole had said.

"I'm sorry, Tony."

He looked back at Cole, shaking his head to dismiss it. "Nah. Let's not even go there."

Shifting his legs around and pulling his arms even tighter around his chest, Tony returned to staring out at the North Atlantic. Never one to feel uncomfortable in silence, Cole now wished that Tony would say anything. He could no longer feel his feet as he tried unsuccessfully to wiggle his toes. The only response was a sharp burning pain. He shuddered and tried to not think about what the night had in store for them.

Looking up at the fog, Cole let go of any hope and focused on his breathing. He'd been here before, far too many times to count. Reaching down for the bottle of water, he took a small sip, perhaps only an ounce, before handing it over to Tony, telling him, "Take a sip."

"I'm good."

Cole pressed the jug at him. "It's better if you take small sips spaced out over time."

Reaching out with his trembling hand, Tony took it and raised the jug to his lips, trying hard not to spill any as he took a sip. Spinning the cap back on tight, he set it down in the center of the raft and took a breath. "We all gotta die someday."

Cole looked at him, thinking for a moment before he replied, "Better this than in Velcro shoes and a diaper."

Tony laughed for the first time since they'd been in the raft. He shivered some more, then continued laughing as they looked at each other.

"You may be right, Cole."

As the evening approached and the greyness around them darkened even more, Cole thought only of the silence around them. The sea was eerily calm, a smooth plane of glass in every direction that seemed endlessly intertwined with the sky above. He looked at Tony who was now clearly in bad shape from exposure. A sadness set in, leading Cole to look down and away from his friend. It was tragic and beautiful at the same time.

A faint rumble caught his attention, and he looked up at Tony, who had lifted his head as well and looked off in the distance. A moment later, Tony turned and stared in the other direction, a look of confusion on his face as he shuddered hard. Cole stared at him until Tony turned and the two looked at each other. The rumble grew louder, and Cole let half a smile sneak out. Tony shivered and looked again to his side,

Cole still staring at him. Tony's eyes narrowed, and he craned his head away before a look of disbelief took hold. Cole smiled.

Finally, turning his attention outside the raft and towards the increasing roar above the fog, Cole saw it for himself. From less than a mile away, the sound grew in intensity as several bright lights pierced the fog from above. A moment later, the hulking white and orange outline of a C-130 broke through the overcast layer and seemed to skim the surface of the water. Cole smiled so hard that the skin of his chapped laps cracked as it passed overhead with a deafening roar, no more than 50 feet above them.

Still in disbelief, Tony asked, "What are they doing?"

Calmly, and with indifference, Cole replied, "They're saving us, Tony."

ABOUT THE AUTHOR

BRIAN BOLAND is a 2003 graduate of the United States Coast Guard Academy and holds a Master of Arts in Military History from Norwich University. After an initial assignment at sea, he completed Naval Flight Training and was designated a Coast Guard aviator in 2008. With more than a decade of operational experience, he has deployed extensively throughout the Caribbean, Central America, and the eastern Pacific, supporting search and rescue, migrant interdiction, and counter-narcotics missions.

CPSIA information can be obtained
at www.ICGtesting.com
Printed in the USA
FSHW021401220720
71821FS